LAST HERO

TIMOTHY D. MCLENDON

OLYMPUS   ELISIUM   TARTARUS

This book is a work of fiction. Names, characters, places, and incidents are products of the author's imagination. Any resemblance to actual events or locales or persons, living or dead, is entirely coincidental.

Except for Olympus.

ISBN-13: 978-1507810798
ISBN-10: 1507810792

For my son Zander Blaze,

When the time is right, use my fire.

CHAPTER 1
BEACH BIRTHDAY PARTY

"MAKE A wish, Danny," Becky said and smiled. "I hope you get everything you want."

Danny Neumann chuckled at Becky and looked around the room at the dozens of his friends cheering and clapping for him. Most of them were from school, and one was from church. Danny stared down at the sixteen sparkling candles on his vanilla birthday cake with vanilla whipped icing. He didn't believe in wishes, but there was one thing in this room he wanted more than anything else.

Becky lived across the street, and they had been friends since they were four. They knew everything about each other and kept the other's secrets. He had told her years ago he wanted his sixteenth birthday on the beach. She drove him the thirty minutes from Cooper City to this rented Fort Lauderdale beach house tonight and surprised him. She truly was a good friend. Something changed over the last summer break, though. Her big brown eyes pierced his heart every time he looked at her now. Her hair was like golden silk that flowed down the length of her back.

Danny took a deep breath and blew the candles out.

"Where's Kevin?" he asked Becky. Her boyfriend had been his best friend for years until they returned to school from summer break a few months ago. Danny had told Kevin how he was falling in love with Becky and was going to ask her out before school started. Danny was devastated the next day when he found out Kevin had asked Becky to be his girlfriend, and she accepted. Now Kevin acted like he didn't even know Danny. He had lifted weights all summer and grown another foot taller. He only hung out with the popular kids now.

"He had other plans," Becky said, looking away.

Danny shook his head when he realized the truth. Kevin didn't know anything about this party. He probably didn't even remember it was Danny's birthday. Becky wouldn't have reminded him because he would never have allowed her to organize this.

"It wasn't a lie," Becky said. "I told him I had to go out of town to meet some friends."

Danny's face grew hot and turned red, like it always did when he was angry. "I'm going outside for a minute."

"Danny, wait," he heard Becky call after him. He was already at the sliding glass door that led to the back porch and couldn't turn around. He hated for her to see him like this. He opened the door to the sounds of crashing waves in the near distance.

"Better get your boyfriend," Danny heard someone tell Becky. He turned and saw that it was Becky's friend Marc. He was a short Asian kid with spiked hair. He always talked in a high-pitched voice and wore make up.

Becky laughed. "We're just friends, Marc."

"Sure you are." He winked at her.

Danny's face felt even hotter. He closed the door and raced toward the beach. He had to get away from all of this. This was not how he'd imagined his sixteenth birthday.

"Slow down," Becky screamed after him. He heard the sliding glass door close again. She ran up behind him and tackled him in the sand. "You can't run away every time you're scared of something. Not with those chicken legs."

"I'm not scared." He sat up and ran his fingers through the sand like a fork.

Becky sat next to him and leaned against his shoulder. "I've known you most of my life, Danny Neumann. And this is exactly what you do when you're scared."

He wrapped an arm around her shoulder and looked into her big brown eyes. He hesitated. "Why can't we be together?"

"Maybe if things were different…" She sighed. He could tell she was lost in thought when she folded her hands under her chin and stared straight ahead. "We're always there for each other. Isn't that enough?"

"I'm in love with you."

Becky took Danny's arm off her shoulder. She spoke slower than normal, "I love you to death, and you'll always have a piece of my heart." She stood and grabbed a handful of sand. "But you're just too boring." She threw the sand at him and ran away laughing toward the water.

"What does that even mean?" he shouted after her.

"Can't catch me, Chicken Legs!"

"Oh, yeah?" He jumped up, cleared his pockets, threw his cell phone down, and raced after her. Her feet were already in the water. She walked backward and wriggled her fingers at him, daring him to catch her.

He ran in and tackled her the same way she had tackled him. They were at waist level in the water now. They both popped their heads out of the water and laughed.

Becky splashed some water in his face. "You wear the same clothes, eat the same food, and go to bed at the same time every night. Even your birthday cake is plain."

Danny never liked change. "At least I don't forget to shave my hairy legs."

Becky smirked. "You shave your legs?"

"Not me!" Danny splashed water back at her. "You!" Her drenched hair lay straight down behind her. Her eyes sparkled in the reflection of the water. Her shirt was snug against her body, showing her shapely form.

She pursed her lips and batted her eyes. "Leave my legs out of this. What did they ever do to you?" She cleared her throat and moved in closer to him. "Maybe one day things will be different."

I knew wishes were worthless.

"We should head back inside," Becky said, staring up at the sky. "It looks like there's a storm coming."

Danny agreed, when he noticed the sky had darkened and a distant roar bellowed from the ocean. They stepped out of the water and headed back up the beach toward the deck. He opened the sliding glass door when they got there, and let Becky in first.

"Put on a smile and let's have some fun, Danny."

"Sure. What else am I going to do with my boring life?"

"Happy birthday, Danny."

HALF OF the birthday cake was gone. It looked lonely and naked sitting on the table with only the word 'Happy' left stranded across the top half. Danny's friends danced around the room to loud techno music with paper plates full of cake crumbs. A few of them gulped down cans of beer.

"Hey, girl," Marc said to Becky. "I see you got your man."

Becky looked at Danny and mouthed *I'm sorry*. "I think you've had too much to drink, Marc. Kevin is my boyfriend."

Marc winked at Danny. "This is club soda," he said, holding up his red plastic cup. "It doesn't take beer goggles to see that you two are wet for each other." He clicked his tongue and turned around. "Time to get my dance on!"

Danny couldn't move. He didn't realize anyone knew how he felt about Becky. It didn't help that they were the only two people soaking wet. If word got out to Kevin then there would be trouble.

"I'm going to dry off and see if I can find other clothes for us," Becky said. She reached behind her and grabbed her hair then wringed it like a wet towel. Water splashed all over the floor. "And I'll get a mop." She smiled and headed for another room.

Danny watched her walk away and imagined what it would be like if they were together. Kevin always took her to fast food restaurants and movies, and got her roses on her birthday. But those weren't things Becky liked. She liked the fresh scent of yellow carnations. She always wanted to go to a rock concert and jam with the group backstage. Her favorite food was mint chocolate chip ice cream.

"Hey, Lover Boy," someone said.

Danny turned to see Marc standing in front of him again. He had a devilish smile on his face and shook his head. "You've got it bad."

Marc pointed to the front room by the door. "Some scary old guy is asking for you. His nails are dirty, and his hair is a jungle. But I'm not one to judge." He swayed his shoulders from side to side and snapped his fingers when the music changed. "That's my song!"

Danny stepped through the crowd. Several guys fist pumped him and wished him, "Happy birthday!" He didn't really know most of the kids at the party. Becky had probably convinced them to come for the beer. Truth was, he only had a handful of friends, and they came from both sides of the spectrum.

"Can I help you?" Danny said when he entered the front room. An old man in a trench coat faced the door. He carried a top hat in his right hand. He was the tallest man Danny had ever seen. The guy's head nearly touched the ceiling.

Danny lost his breath when the man turned around. His face was a mask of grooves and pock marks. His eyes were pitch black.

"Hello, Alexandros Helen." His voice was the deepest Danny had ever heard. It echoed through the room like thunder.

Danny swallowed hard. His stomach churned. He had no idea who Alexandros Helen was. "You have me confused with someone else," he heard himself say in a raspy whisper. "My name is Danny Neumann."

The man threw his head back and laughed. His chortles bounced off the walls like a drum solo. "Neumann? That's what they told you?"

Danny tried to breathe at an even pace. He wanted to run but somehow knew this man would never let him get away. "I need to get back to my party."

The old man shook his head and widened his eyes. "It's a shame your parents aren't alive to see this."

Danny stopped breathing. He saw his parents just a few hours ago. They couldn't be dead. "What are you saying? Who are you?"

"You can call me Ty." He put his hat on and stepped toward Danny. "I've waited sixteen years for this. It's time for the last descendant to die."

Ty reached out, extending long, bony, filthy fingers. Danny flinched.

He felt a surge of energy build as his body tightened, and his fingers clawed into his palms. He yelled and threw his hands out to release the energy. A ball of light shot out from his hands and slammed into Ty's body.

The old man was thrown back and crashed into the wall. He slumped and fell face-first.

Danny stared at his hands. He turned them over and flexed them, studying the appendages like he had never seen them before. He had no idea what just happened. He felt stronger than he ever had. Invincible.

Ty stood back up and glared at him. His eyes seemed to move from side to side like he was confused. He cracked his neck and rolled his shoulders back. "I will defeat you."

"What's going on in here?" Marc called out as he stepped into the room. "It sounds like all hell broke loose."

Danny held out his hands for Marc to stay where he was. He turned to protect him from Ty, but the old man was gone. The front door was wide open, and the dark, rainy night stared back at him.

"Everything okay?" Marc asked.

Danny panicked when he patted his pockets and realized he had left his phone on the beach. He raced over to Marc. "Give me your phone."

Marc stared at him. "Seriously? Where are your manners?"

Danny jammed his hand into Marc's pocket and yanked the phone out. There wasn't any time to explain.

Marc put his hands up. "Okay, that's new. I thought you were playing for the other team."

Danny dialed his home phone number. His parents couldn't be dead. The old man was trying to scare him for some reason. The phone rang and rang. "Please pick up. Please pick up." His hands trembled.

Becky stood next to Marc. "What's going on?"

"I think he's mad we ate his cake."

Danny threw the phone back to Marc. It bounced off his chest and fell to the floor. "I need your car right now, Becky."

"Okay. Calm down." She stepped up to him and cupped his hands. "You're shaking. I've never seen you like this. What's wrong?"

"My parents are in trouble."

Becky searched his eyes then grabbed her purse. "Let's go."

CHAPTER 2
NO STEROIDS NEEDED

KEVIN SKINNER lay on his Olympic weight bench, sucked in as much air as he could, and grabbed the barbell above him in a wide overhand grip. He pressed up in an attempt to bench two hundred and thirty pounds for the first time. His personal best was two hundred and twenty. He grunted and strained, but the bar wouldn't move.

"Frickin A!"

He let go of the bar and rested on the bench for a minute. He had reached his natural potential. Three months ago he lay here and could barely press the forty-five pound bar by itself. He hated his former weak pathetic scrawny self at one hundred and thirty pounds. Now he was one hundred and sixty-five pounds of Grade A muscle.

Kevin didn't have time for anyone who didn't try to build the best body they could. Those kinds of people didn't have enough respect for themselves. People like Danny Neumann. Sure, Danny was a good guy, and they'd had good times together, but he would always be a pathetic loser. He could have asked Becky out, but Kevin liked her, too. Danny should have asked.

Kevin sat up and flexed his chest. *Who's the man? I'm the man!*

"You'll get it next time," Susan said. Kevin had invited her over to watch him workout in his garage. She purred and ran a hand over his rippled chest.

Kevin grasped her arm and pulled her onto his lap. He kissed her deeply. Sure, every guy at school had been with her, but she had one smoking body with her long legs and double D chest. The old Kevin could never get a girl like this. The new improved Kevin could get everything he deserved.

"Bet your girlfriend never let you do this." She put his hand on her chest. Second base! "You like that, don't you?"

Kevin pulled her in closer. She was right. Becky barely let him get past first base. She was always so obsessed about being a proper lady. The new Kevin deserved more than a boring relationship like that. But he would never let Becky go. It was only right to keep a beautiful girl like her away from a pathetic loser like Danny.

The garage door opened. Darkness and water seeped in.

Kevin reached over to the garage remote and pressed the button to close the door. It wouldn't respond. As the door rose he thought he could see a body on the other side standing there, waiting for him.

An old man stared back at him when the door was fully raised. He was a mountain of a man and the ugliest Kevin had ever seen. Water splashed all over the concrete when he took two steps into the garage.

"I can make you stronger," the old man said.

"I didn't think you'd ever get here," Kevin replied. Joe, the biggest kid at school, said he'd hook him up with a good steroid dealer. He'd been waiting for 2 weeks and had more than a thousand dollars set aside for this.

Kevin pushed Susan out of his lap and stood. "Get out of here," he said to her.

"But it's raining!"

"Get out of here!"

Susan slapped him and ran out of the garage. "Don't ever call me again!"

The garage door closed as soon as she ran out. Kevin looked at the remote in his hand. He hadn't pressed it.

"I don't want a limp noodle or big boobs," Kevin said. One of the guys at school got a limp noodle from Deca and another got big boobs from D-bol. Kevin just wanted something to make him bigger and stronger without any side effects.

The old man cracked his neck. Water crept down his long gray hair and splashed in little drops on the floor. "Alexandros Helen must die."

Kevin froze. What the hell was the old guy talking about? He had to be crazy, and must've wandered from off the streets. "Joe didn't send you, did he?"

The old man stared at him like an ant. "Alexandros doesn't know who he is yet. He can't control his powers."

Kevin snatched a dumbbell bar off the floor and took a wide stance. "I don't know who Alexandros is, and I don't know who you are. But if you don't get out of here, I'm going to kick your ass."

The man laughed. "Alexandros calls himself Danny Neumann. You can call me Ty."

Kevin loosened his grip on the dumbbell bar. What did Danny have to do with this? What the hell was going on here?

"He tried to hurt me, but he only made me stronger," Ty said. He shot an arm out toward Kevin and tightened his fist.

Kevin couldn't breathe. He felt like his throat was being crushed. His feet lifted off the floor like he was floating. He could see the old man was lower than him now.

"I have no use for this power," the old man said. "I cannot hurt Alexandros because the rules have changed. But a human can. You can." His put his arm down and Kevin collapsed to the floor.

Kevin stood and gasped for air. This man was more powerful than any steroid could ever make him. Kevin would do anything to be as strong as him. "How can I—"

The old man reached for Kevin's shoulders and held them in a vice grip. Energy surged through Kevin's body like electricity. The room spun in circles, and his head felt like it would explode.

He crumpled on the floor when Ty released his grip. The world turned black.

"You will kill Alexandros Helen," he heard a faint voice say. "And you will have everything you want."

KEVIN AWOKE to the pitter patter of rain on concrete. His back ached from lying on the garage floor. He sat up and waited for his head to stop spinning. When it cleared, he remembered what the old man had promised him.

Kevin stood and laughed. Had he been drinking? Was the whole thing just a dream? Had Susan been here and let him feel up her shirt? He sure hoped so!

Kevin strode to his Olympic weight bench and prepared to press the two hundred and thirty pounds again. "Please work." He took a deep breath and pressed the bar up without any effort.

"Amazing!"

He lowered the bar to his chest and pushed it back up ten times before putting it back in the rack. His heart still beat at the same rate, and he wasn't even breathing hard.

He took one hand off the bar and centered the other on the bar. "It's not possible," he said. "Or is it?" He pressed the two hundred and thirty pounds up with one hand and held it there, then stood up from the bench with the bar still over his head.

He looked outside the garage and tossed the bar toward the driveway. It flew out of his hand and landed at the end of the driveway. Chunks of concrete shot up into the air.

"Alexandros Helen is Danny Neumann." Kevin sat on the weight bench and put his hands on his head. "Danny must die."

CHAPTER 3
STRUCK BY LIGHTNING

DANNY'S HANDS wouldn't stop shaking. He fumbled with the house keys over and over. Every time he gripped one it slipped out of his fingers.

Becky snatched the keys from him and shoved the right one into the keyhole. She threw the door open and raced inside. "Mr. and Mrs. Neumann? Hello?" She ran from room to room.

Danny stood in the doorway. He was afraid that if he took one more step forward he might discover the truth—that his parents really were dead. He shivered as the rain pelted his back.

"What's all this ruckus?" his mom shouted, walking out of the kitchen. She wiped butter off her hands on the rose designed apron he got her for her birthday. Her long brown hair was tied back in a bun.

Danny couldn't help but cry. He didn't recall ever being this relieved.

"Get out of that rain, boy," his dad said. He poked his head out of the kitchen with a chicken leg in his hand. His glasses drooped down his nose. "You've got more sense than that."

Danny wiped the tears from his face and stepped inside. He was grateful his parents were alive, but something kept nagging him as he looked at them. Something wasn't right.

"He said you were dead."

"Who said that?" his dad asked.

His mom ran up to him and wrapped her arms around his shoulders. She closed the door behind them. "It's okay. We're right here." She guided him to the couch and sat next to him.

Danny didn't know if they'd believe what he had to tell them about Ty. He wasn't sure if he believed it himself. "He said my name isn't Neumann."

Danny watched his mom look up at his dad. They stared at each other a minute until his dad nodded. Danny knew they had something to tell him, and it wouldn't be good.

"Becky," his mom said, "there's some chicken and mashed potatoes in the kitchen. You should help yourself."

Becky looked at him with wide eyes. They locked eyes for a moment, and he wondered if she could see his soul. She walked away when he nodded at her.

"Danny," his dad said, "you need to tell us everything."

Danny didn't think he could but when his mom's smile reassured him, he couldn't help but tell them everything that happened with Ty. He expected them to laugh at him and maybe call the asylum downtown. Instead, his dad paced the room.

"This wasn't supposed to happen!" his dad yelled. He punched the wall.

Danny's mom sighed. Her eyes were fixed on the wall like she was in a daze. "We knew this day could come. We just didn't want it to."

Danny's hands trembled. His parents always had the answers, but they seemed lost for the first time. "What? What's going on?"

His dad crossed his arms and put his head down.

"We've been here since the day you were born," his mom said. "You'll always be our son." She stopped for a minute and took a deep breath. The room was silent, and Danny wasn't sure if she would say anything else. "But the names of your birth parents are Margaret and Thomas Helen."

"No," Danny said. "That's not true. Don't try to scare me."

His dad walked up to him and put a hand on his shoulder. Tears glistened in his eyes; Danny had never seen his dad cry. That's how he knew it was all true.

Danny couldn't look at his parents. Why had they hidden this from him? They should have told him earlier. Now what was he supposed to do? His whole life was a lie.

"Thomas Helen was my best friend," his dad said. "He was a good man. He asked us to take care of you if anything ever happened to him and Margaret."

"What happened? Where are they?" Becky peeked out of the kitchen. Her brown eyes were full of sorrow.

His mom took another deep breath. "I'm sorry, Danny. They're not alive."

Danny stood up. "I don't believe you."

"Sit down, boy," his dad said. He pointed to the main bedroom. "Mary, go get the article."

Danny's mom stood, wringing her hands. "Are you sure? He needs more time."

His dad nodded.

His mom bunched her apron, pulled it up, and wiped her face in it. She walked away slower than he had ever seen her. Her normally vibrant arms hung by her side.

His dad sat next to him and stared at the floor. "Thomas Helen chose us to be your parents. He chose our name—Neumann." He stood back up to let Danny's mom sit down as she came back into the room. "That's got to mean something."

His mom handed him a laminated newspaper article. It slid out of her hand like she didn't have the strength to hold it, and fell right into Danny's lap. He stared down at the words screaming at him.

COUPLE STRUCK BY LIGHTNING was the article title. Danny glanced over it. He saw the names Thomas and Margaret Helen. It said their bodies were burned beyond recognition, and dental records had to be used for identification. But then he saw the one thing that let him know his parents were lying. He was surprised they had missed something so simple in such an elaborate hoax.

"This article was written November 19, 1998. That just happens to be my birthday." He glanced at Becky in the kitchen. "Is this a joke? Are you in on this?"

Becky shook her head.

"Margaret Helen was 6 months pregnant when she died," his mom said.

Danny threw his arms up and laughed. "You expect me to believe I was born 3 months early out of a charred cadaver?"

His mom smiled at him. "You were born without a scratch."

CHAPTER 4
FOLLOW THE STARS

DANNY STORMED out of the house and slammed the door. The rain had stopped, and the sky was the darkest he had ever seen it. The only light came from the carport. He carried his telescope by his side and sloshed through the mud for the open area over the septic mound in the back yard.

"Danny, wait," he heard Becky scream after him.

He turned and held out a hand. "I can't do this right now. Please leave me alone."

Becky had tears in her eyes. "I'm here for you, Danny. Don't shut me out."

Danny threw his telescope down and marched up to her. His birth parents were dead. His best friend didn't want anything to do with him. The girl he loved was with someone else. "You have no idea how this feels. No one wants me."

Becky grabbed his hands and spoke slowly. "I know you're hurting, but don't ever say that again. I will always be here for you, Danny Neumann."

Danny's face turned red. "Why didn't you choose me?"

Becky's face froze, and she seemed to stop breathing. "It's not that easy. Call me when you're ready to talk. I'll see you tomorrow, Danny." She took two steps back then turned and walked toward her car.

Danny wanted to race after her. He had yelled at her, maybe even scared her, and he was sorry for it. But he had to let her go no matter how much it hurt. She could never love someone like him. No one could love him.

Danny snatched his telescope out of the mud and headed for the septic mound. It was the one place where he had a clear view of the night sky. He had watched the stars from there since he was six years old. The stars were the only things that made his world feel centered and at peace.

He set the telescope tripod up and searched the sky for the zodiac. He soon found the Ursa Minor constellation and focused on Polaris. Most people called it the Northern Star. It was the forty-fifth brightest star. Something about Polaris always calmed him down.

"You're looking at the Northern Star again, aren't you?" he heard his mom's voice ask.

Danny never took his eye off the telescope. "I don't have anything to say to you." He heard her sigh then step up to him and set something by his feet.

"You don't have to say anything. Just listen." She sighed again and put a hand on his shoulder. "Your birth mother loved you more than anything in the world."

Danny gulped. He wanted to hear more.

"She and your birth father came over for dinner a few times. I was jealous of her because she was such a beautiful woman." She laughed. "She always talked about you and how much she wanted to give you a good life."

Danny looked up from the telescope. "Was she a good person?"

His mom smiled. "Yes. You have a lot of her personality."

"Am I like my birth father?"

"Yes. He was an honest man. I think he would have given his life to save a total stranger."

Danny faced his mom and cried. "What am I?" He couldn't get the flash of light out of his mind. How had he sent out a burst of energy that stopped the old man? "And who is Ty?"

"Listen to me," his mom said. "I don't know who Ty is, but I do know that you're my son. We'll figure this out together."

Danny took a deep breath and nodded. He knew this woman loved him, and everything she said was true.

His mom pointed to the ground near the telescope. A green notebook lay there. "That's for you."

Danny reached down and snatched it. He opened it to the first page and looked at penciled drawings of constellations. He turned through the pages to find the entire book was full of hand drawings with coordinates.

"You wrote this?" he asked his mom. She had never shown any interest in the stars.

"It took me 5 years. I've never shown it to anyone."

Danny looked back up at her. It didn't make any sense.

She stared at him for a minute then looked up into the sky. "Your birth parents were fascinating people. They told us unbelievable stories about their lives." She looked back at him and smiled. "You might want to sit down."

DANNY LISTENED to every word his mom had to say. Right now he wanted to know everything about his birth parents and find out who or what he was.

"The last page of the notebook has something you should look at," his mom said.

Danny shuffled through the pages of constellations and star charts. The last page was full of numbers. He recognized them as coordinates in the Ursa Minor.

"Go ahead and look at the sky."

Danny went back to his telescope and searched for the two coordinates on the paper. He had no idea why it made any difference. He knew all the stars by heart.

"Your birth parents asked us to take care of you if anything happened to them. But they also said they would watch over you."

Danny blinked and double checked the coordinates he was looking at. He stared at two stars that had never been there before.

"This isn't possible," Danny said. "I know all of the stars." He couldn't take his eyes off of them. Polaris helped illuminate them like they had always been there. He looked back at his mom. "You discovered two new stars. You're going to be famous."

She laughed. "They're not new stars. They've been there for exactly sixteen years."

Danny crossed his arms. "I don't understand."

She stepped up to him and wrapped an arm around his shoulders. "Those two stars are only visible on November 19. They're completely dark every other night."

"What does it mean?"

She took her arm off his shoulders and put her face in front of his. "I think I always believed it but refused to accept it until tonight." She hesitated. "Your birth parents once said that if they died then they would be placed as stars in heaven to watch over you."

Danny would have laughed an hour ago, but there they were, in the sky shining down on him. "It doesn't make any sense."

His mom nodded slowly and stared into his eyes. "They said they would be placed there as a promise from the gods."

"What?"

"I don't know what it means. But I do know you're not like everyone else. You're a gift from heaven."

CHAPTER 5
SPEAKING OF THE ENEMY

BECKY DIDN'T know if she couldn't see the road clearly because of her tears or because of the drizzle of rain on the windshield. Danny was her best friend, and she couldn't stand to see him hurting the way he was. She wished she could tell him how much she wanted to be with him.

She remembered the first day he moved into town. They were both five years old at the time. Danny had the deepest blue eyes she had ever seen. She knew right away they would be friends for life and told him as much.

It seemed like they were closer than ever this past summer. Danny swam with her at the city pool every week, and chased her around the pool chairs. They always laughed and held each other for a moment when he caught her. More than once she thought he was going to kiss her, but he never did. Becky was foolish to think that he liked her that way. Danny hadn't even noticed her until after Kevin asked her out.

Becky fished into her jeans pocket and pulled out her cell phone. She pressed Kevin's picture and put the phone to her ear. It rang, but he didn't answer. He was probably out with his friends, but she needed to talk to him now. She headed for his house.

Becky didn't understand why Kevin and Danny couldn't get along. Kevin said it was because Danny thought he was better than him. Danny said it was because Kevin thought he was better than everyone. After tonight, she didn't know what to believe anymore.

She pulled into Kevin's driveway and jerked when her car hit something hard. She slammed her brakes, jumped out of the car, and raced to the front fender, scared she had hit an animal. It took a moment for her eyes to adjust to the object just beneath the headlights. It looked like one of Kevin's weights.

"Hey," Kevin said, walking out of the garage, "what are you doing here?"

Becky crossed her arms. "What is this? I'm gonna have to check my tires."

Kevin kicked one of the tires. "They're fine, babe. I was just getting in a good workout outside."

"In the rain?"

"I live life dangerously."

Becky chuckled. "I need to talk to you."

Kevin nodded. "Back your car up and I'll move the barbell. Meet you in the garage."

Becky kissed his cheek. "Thank you for being here for me." She jumped back into her car and backed it up. She watched as Kevin picked up the barbell. He looked bigger and more muscular than she remembered. He must have gotten a really good pump from his workout.

"What'd you want to talk about?" Kevin said when she joined him in the garage. He was doing curls and staring at his biceps.

"Oh, nothing." Maybe this wasn't a good idea. She didn't want to stir any more bad blood between Kevin and Danny.

Kevin put his weights down. "Come on, now. I know you were at Danny's party. You wouldn't have driven all the way back here for nothing." His perfect smile warmed her heart. He was always so perceptive and understanding. He was the perfect man.

"Promise not to get mad?" Becky said.

"I could never be mad at the prettiest girl in town."

Becky blushed. "It's been a rough night."

Kevin stood and put an arm around her. His embrace was comforting. "You came to the right place. What happened?"

"Danny found out some news that hurt him." She sighed. "Danny was adopted. His real name is Alexandros Helen. I don't know how to help him."

Kevin sat her down. "Maybe I can help. Tell me all about it."

CHAPTER 6
EXPLODING TRASH

DANNY STOOD in the morning fog at 5:15 A.M. and squinted every time a car with blurry headlights passed by. The air was chilly, but he sensed only warmth. He covered his head with the hood of his sweatshirt and began the two mile jog he took every morning.

He stopped when the loud engine of a dirty white van crept by his side. The man in the passenger seat stared at him and waved. The van sped away after a few seconds. Danny noticed the tag was from Los Angeles, California. *You're a long ways from home.*

Danny resumed his pace and thought about how he had lain in bed all night, with his hands clasped behind his head, while he stared at the white popcorn ceiling. He pictured each bump in the ceiling as the people he saw yesterday. There was Becky, Kevin, Marc, Ty, his parents, and two stars. How did they all fit together?

And what about Becky? She had seemed upset when she left last night. He felt bad and wanted to apologize. He had seen her only hours ago and missed her already, missed the way she looked, the way she smiled, the way she made him feel like a better person. His stomach cramped in anger when he thought about it.

Butterflies in my stomach? More like daggers!

Danny stopped when he reached the city park and looked around in confusion. He must have been lost in thoughts because it seemed like he had just left from the house. He hadn't even broken a sweat. He glanced at his watch and saw that it was 5:17 A.M. He tapped on the watch.

Two miles in two minutes? Must be broken, he thought.

Danny headed for one of the four racquetball courts. Each one was like a cement fortress, perfect for what he needed. He seized one of the city's garbage cans in the park and toted it to the court. He unlatched the metal door to Court 3 and shoved the garbage can inside with him. Danny looked around to make sure no one was watching and closed the door behind him.

He rolled the garbage can to the front wall and centered it. He walked back to the entrance door, jumped up and down, and stretched his arms and calves. He didn't have a stringed racquet or hollow rubber ball, but all he needed for this were his hands.

Danny stared at the garbage can like it was an enemy he had to destroy. He put one leg in front of the other and threw his hands out toward the can. He waited for a ball of energy to crush it.

Nothing happened.

Okay, he thought, *I've got this*.

He jumped up and down a few more times then spread his legs in a sumo stance. He peeled his sweatshirt off so his arms were loose. He concentrated all of his energy on the can and threw out his hands again.

Nothing happened.

"Why isn't this working?" He rubbed his head and paced the court. The answer came to him when he looked at the garbage can again. "Because you're not a crazy person trying to kill me. You're just a stupid garbage can."

He laughed and walked up to the can. He pushed it back toward the entrance but stopped. "The least I can do is kick you in the balls." He kicked it right between its wheels.

The can flew across the court and exploded against the entrance wall. Garbage shot out and rained on half the court.

Danny stood there and stared at the garbage. He blinked and tried to figure out how any of this was possible. Just yesterday he hated taking out the trash because it was so heavy.

Sunlight began to fill the court. Danny looked at his watch and saw that it was after 6 A.M. He wanted to get home before his parents knew he was out. He walked back to the entrance and opened the metal door.

The dirty white van that had passed him earlier was parked parallel to the court, its engine choking and gurgling. The passenger door opened and a man in a black suit and shades stepped out. He looked to be thirty years old.

"Danny Neumann?" the man said, walking toward him.

Danny didn't take his eyes off the man. He had no idea who the guy was. He felt an energy building inside him, the same energy he'd felt when Ty attacked him.

The driver's door opened and a large man appeared. He clasped his hands behind his back.

"Don't be afraid," the man in the black suit said. He took off his shades and held his hands out. Both of his palms had a tattoo of a blue oval, like a saucer.

"I don't want any trouble," Danny said. "Stay away from me." He scanned the park for the quickest escape route. He could fight this man if he had to.

The man put his shades back on. "It looks like we're gonna have to do this the hard way." He snapped his fingers.

Danny caught a glimpse of the driver raising his hands over the hood. There was something in his hands. *What is that? Is that a gun?*

Danny heard a puff then felt a sting in his neck. He grabbed his neck and pulled a dart from his skin. He tried to look at it, but the world was blurry. "What is this?"

The man stepped toward him. "That's enough tranquilizers to take out a team of horses."

Danny felt like the world was spinning. He wouldn't be able to stand much longer. Why were they doing this to him?

"Don't worry, Danny boy," the man said. "If I'm right about you, this will only knock you out for a few minutes."

Danny tried to throw his hands out and attack the man, but he couldn't move. "If you're right? What if you're wrong?"

"I sure hope not, Danny boy." He slapped Danny's face. "If I'm wrong then you're about to die."

CHAPTER 7
SUIT MAN WEARS DIRTY SOCKS

DANNY TRIED to move his hands, but they were behind his back and bound with duct tape. His entire body felt exhausted. "What do you want with me?"

The man in the black suit stared straight ahead. "Don't bother. Your hands are secured for our protection."

Danny observed cars passing by from the passenger window to this right, and knew the men had trapped him in the backseat of the dirty white van. He searched for a street sign or business, any kind of landmark. He realized they were still on Main Street, driving at a crawl. "Where are you taking me?"

The man turned and faced Danny. "You don't get to ask questions. One more word and I'll take my sock off and stuff it down your throat. Got it?"

The driver pulled to a side street that led to the city landfill. Instinctively, Danny knew they were going to bury him alive. He concentrated on his hands and tried to generate some kind of energy from them. Now would be a good time for his power to work.

The van stopped when they reached the landfill entrance. No one was around except for the vultures eating rotten food for breakfast. The driver took his key out of the ignition and turned to face the man in the suit.

"You wore the same socks yesterday," the driver said. "Disgusting."

"Shut up, Al," the man in the suit said.

Al held up his hands. "Hey! No names!"

Suit Man brushed him off and stared at Danny. "You're going to do something for us."

Danny felt energy building up inside of him that needed to be released. Instead of fear, he felt anger. "Let me go, and I won't hurt you."

Al banged his fist on the steering wheel. "I told you this wouldn't work."

"Shut up, Al," Suit Man said. He redirected his attention to Danny and held out a file folder. "Your mom seems like a nice old lady. Goes to work every morning at 7:30. She takes the scenic route to her job at a flower shop. Your old man leaves an hour later to volunteer at the Veteran's Hospital." He paused and shook his head. "These are good people. I'd hate to see anything bad happen to them."

Danny struggled to break loose. "I'll kill you if you touch them." How long had these men been watching his family? And why?

Suit Man closed his eyes and shook his head. "Danny boy, I don't think you could hurt a fly. But I think you better learn how to real quick." He put a hand on Danny's shoulder. "You're going to bring us the head of the cosmic master."

Danny somehow knew who Suit Man was talking about. "Ty," he whispered.

Suit man smiled and nodded. "Smart kid."

Danny's head swam in confusion. He still didn't know who Ty was and now these men wanted him dead. Wait, he didn't even know who these men were. "You're going to answer some questions first."

"He's got balls," the driver said.

Suit Man glared at the driver. "Shut up and start driving." The driver sighed, cranked the van on, and turned the white heap of junk around.

"Two questions," Suit Man said.

Danny's mind raced. He had a million questions. He tried to think of the two that would help make the most sense out of this. "Who are you?"

Suit Man leaned back. "We belong to a society that protects the world from destruction by extraterrestrial intelligences."

Danny couldn't breathe. This could be the key to finding his purpose and making sense of last night. All he had to do was ask who he was.

"One more question," Suit Man reminded him.

Danny wanted to ask about his origins, but he knew the question he had to ask to save his parents. "How do I find Ty?"

Suit man smirked. "You surprise me, Danny boy. As for Ty, he'll find you."

The van slowed to a stop. Danny looked out his widow and saw that his house was across the street. Suit Man opened the van door and reached for Danny's shoulders.

"Don't get any bright ideas," Suit Man said. "If you tell anyone about us, I'll kill your parents. If you don't bring us Ty's head, I'll kill your parents. Just act like everything's normal and have fun today." He cut the duct tape from Danny's hands and tossed him out of the van. "We'll be watching you."

Danny stood there as the van peeled down the road. "Wait," he shouted. "Who am I?"

CHAPTER 8
MOVING ON

THE FRONT door to his parents' house opened before Danny could turn the knob. His mom stood there with her hair hanging low and frazzled.

"Danny," she said. "Thank God." She wrapped her arms around him and pulled him in. "Don't ever run off like that again." She stuck her head out the door and surveyed the neighborhood before shutting the door back and locking it.

Danny couldn't help but feel lost in the empty living room. Boxes were lined up against the walls. The furniture was pushed away. It looked like someone was either moving in or moving out.

"What's going on?" Danny asked.

His dad stepped into the room with his arms full of boxes. "Get your stuff together," he said. "We're leaving in three hours."

Danny couldn't move. They couldn't leave—not before he could deal with Ty. His parents had no idea how much trouble they would be in if they left, and Danny couldn't tell them.

"Wait a minute," Danny said. He rubbed his chin and held a hand out for his parents to stop what they were doing. "We're not going anywhere."

His dad dropped the boxes in his arms. "Do what we say, Danny. We know what's best."

"Do you?" Danny said, standing in front of his dad now. He had a mental flash of the newspaper article his mom had given him last night. He didn't notice it at the time, but the article was written in Fort Lewis, Washington. That's where he was born, though his birth certificate said otherwise. His parents had hidden him and run away to Cooper City. Now they wanted to run away again.

He turned and faced his mom. "It doesn't matter where we go. Ty will find me." Danny realized that Ty would never stop until Danny was dead. Somehow Ty could sense him. Running away wouldn't do any good…it never did.

"We have to try," his mom said. "It's our job to protect you."

Danny shook his head. "Not anymore." His mom looked as defeated as she had been when she told him who he was. Her hair was oily, and wrinkles crowded her eyes. "It's my job to protect you now."

"You don't have to do this, Danny," she said, standing by his side. "Your dad and I talked about it. We can start over somewhere else."

He shook his head. "Whatever's happening to me has already happened." He put his hands in front of him and stared at his palms. "I need you to trust me. I can't explain it, but I know I'll be okay."

"We know you will," his dad said. He stood on Danny's other side and put a hand on his shoulder. "You've always been okay. You're not like everyone else. You've never had a broken bone. You've never even had a cold or the flu."

Danny had never thought about it. His whole life he had watched his friends and family get sick, but he had never had a sniffle or needed medicine. He only went to the doctor for checkups.

"We can't let him go," his mom said. "It's too dangerous."

Danny knew it was only dangerous if he didn't take any action. "I've been running away from things my entire life. I can't run anymore."

His dad nodded. "He's going to be okay, Mary. Thomas Helen knew it, and we know it, too."

His mom stood back and put a hand on her forehead. "You don't know that for sure. What about that man? He's trying to hurt Danny for some reason."

Danny stood in front of her and put his hands on her shoulders. He had to convince her to let him go today. "He can't hurt me. He said something about rules."

His mom turned and looked at him with tears in her eyes. "We can't lose you, Danny. You're our world."

Danny felt like his heart was being ripped out. He believed that Ty couldn't hurt him, but he also knew what Suit Man had demanded. Danny couldn't imagine killing another man, but he also couldn't imagine a man not fighting back. None of that mattered. He would save his parents.

"Let him go," his dad said. He winked at Danny. "We believe in you."

Danny nodded at him.

His mom threw up her arms. "There's no way you'll make it to school on time by foot. I'll drive you."

Danny scratched his neck. "I'm pretty sure I can make it in plenty of time."

CHAPTER 9
PLAYING DEAD

DANNY STOOD in front of Cooper City Performing Arts High School and watched the teenagers gathered in cliques outside getting ready for the day. They weren't any different than the cliques at public schools. He still remembered his initial resistance to starting his high school years here. Most of his friends from middle school had gone to the public high school. But now he realized this was the right place for him. The school's purpose was to guide students on their own journey of discovery.

Marc waved at Danny from the crowd. "Hi, Lover Boy," he shouted.

Danny felt his face turning red. He put his head down and marched toward Marc. "Look," he said when he got close to Marc, "I need you to—"

Someone shoved Marc to the ground. Danny saw that it was Joe, the biggest kid at school. He was built like a brick fortress. Everyone knew he was on steroids.

"What's up, faggot?" Joe hovered over Marc.

Danny stood in front of Joe. "Back off, Joe. I don't want to hurt you."

Joe stared at Danny with raised eyebrows. He seemed confused, but then he laughed. "I should have known. You're a faggot too, aren't you?" He shoved Danny down right next to Marc.

"Stay down," Marc whispered. His eyes were closed. "Just play dead. He can't hurt us if we're dead."

Danny looked up at the steroid freak. The kid's face was covered with acne scars and the armpits of his shirt were stained with sweat. Danny wondered how he could beat Ty if he couldn't beat the high school bully.

A crowd gathered around them. "Fight!" one kid shouted.

"Leave them alone," someone said from behind Danny. He turned and saw that it was Kevin.

Joe rubbed his head like he was confused. "You're kidding, right?"

"Leave them alone or you are going to have a problem." He cracked his neck.

Joe beat his hands on his forehead when the In School Suspension (ISS) teacher Ms. Spin walked through the crowd.

"Come with me, Mr. Jones."

Joe beat his fists together and pointed at Kevin. "You called the Five-0 on me? I won't forget this." He shoved students out of the way and followed Ms. Spin inside the school.

Danny felt like his head was swirling. He couldn't understand why Kevin had helped him, when he probably wanted to beat him up himself.

Kevin reached a hand down to help Danny up. He had a wide smile on his face that Danny knew wasn't genuine. It was an expression Kevin had mastered in his acting classes here. Danny stood without Kevin's assistance and helped Marc up.

"Thank you, both," Marc said. "My butt feels bruised but nothing a spa day won't fix." He smiled when Becky joined Kevin's side.

"Are you okay?" she asked Danny and Marc, her eyes moving back and forth. She kissed Kevin's cheek.

Danny nodded. He couldn't look at her. Marc seemed to notice and said, "A grass stain is better than a blood stain. Thank goodness Danny was here." He patted Danny's back and headed inside the school. He pumped his fist in the air and shouted, "Spa day coming up!"

Danny turned to follow Marc. He didn't trust Kevin. He couldn't understand why Becky was with him. "See you inside."

"Danny, wait," Becky said. She grasped his shoulder and tugged on it. "I need to talk to you."

Danny sighed. He couldn't talk to Becky with Kevin by her side flashing that fake smile. "Class is about to start."

"Danny," Kevin said, "I owe you an apology. You've always been a good friend to me, but I haven't been a good one to you."

Danny tried his hardest not to laugh. He recognized that line from a TV movie he'd seen before. Now he knew for sure Kevin was blowing smoke.

"Remember how we used to play video games at my house after school?" Kevin asked. "I've got this great new racing game we can play." He flashed his smile again. "You should come over this afternoon."

"No thanks," Danny said. "I've got other plans."

"Danny, please," Becky said. "Can't you see that Kevin's sorry? I just want the two of you to work things out."

Danny wished Becky could see Kevin the same way that he saw him. Who knew how many lies Kevin had told her? Danny felt sick thinking about how Becky loved Kevin.

"He doesn't love you," Danny said. *I do.*

CHAPTER 10
MR. SILEN HAS A TAIL

DANNY SAT in home room and stared at the blackboard. He didn't sleep last night and the whole morning was a blur. His mom had told him that he was different from everyone else and didn't have to come to school today but he knew he had to go somewhere to help make sense of his life.

"What's the answer, man?"

Danny looked to his right to see Mr. Silen standing over him. He was a big man who always wore jeans and a tie-dye t-shirt with a leather vest over it. His vintage teashade glasses were round with a mirror reflection. Danny looked at his own blank expression staring back at him.

"See me after class, Mr. Neumann," Mr. Silen said. He strode back to the front of the room and turned to face the class. "Don't forget about the Fall Festival tonight. Hay rides, corn maze, games, and lots of candy. It should be super fun."

Danny's eyes widened when he saw Mr. Silen's lower body. It looked like he had a tail and horse legs. Danny rubbed his eyes and laughed. The image was gone. He definitely needed to get some sleep.

Someone tapped him on the shoulder and whispered, "Thirteen."

Danny turned and raised his eyebrows at William Sherman. He was the smartest kid in school with a 4.1 GPA. He had already scored in the 99th percentile on the SATs. He wore beige slacks and a white polo shirt.

"What?"

William smirked and crossed his arms. "It depends on who you ask. Technically there are eight planets and five dwarf planets in our solar system. But that wasn't really the question." He shook his head and laughed.

Danny nodded and laughed with him. He had no idea what William was talking about. "What was the question?"

"Mr. Silen asked you how many planets there are. Most people think there are nine but Pluto has not been considered a planet since 2006. Regardless, to accurately answer the question we have to consider our solar system and all others. Last time I checked, there were four thousand and seventy-one planets and more are discovered every day."

"Sorry I asked." Danny turned back around when the bell rang and chuckled. William was the smartest person he knew, but he was also annoying. No wonder he didn't have any friends.

Danny waited for the room to clear out then snagged his backpack and went to Mr. Silen's desk. The desk was covered in a mess of unorganized papers. "You wanted to see me?"

Mr. Silen leaned back in his chair and sipped out of a thermos he had behind his desk. There were rumors that he was an alcoholic. Danny figured they were probably true because Mr. Silen was always happy and spoke in a slurred retro language that most of the kids found cool.

"Yeah, man. How's life treating you?"

"Okay, I guess."

"Awesome!" Mr. Silen jumped out of his chair and walked to the class door then closed it. He took his glasses off for the first time and Danny saw his bright green eyes. "You saw me, didn't you, Alexandros Helen?"

"How did you know—"

"Listen carefully if you want to walk out of this school alive."

DANNY'S HEART raced and beat against his chest like a hammer. This was the third time someone called him Alexandros Helen. What did this man have in common with Ty? Danny widened his stance and prepared to protect himself.

"I didn't think it was true," Mr. Silen said in a rush.

"What are you talking about?"

Mr. Silen sat back down and took a big gulp from his thermos. He wiped his wet lips on his forearm. "Sixteen years ago something drove us to this city. We didn't know what it was, but the magnetism was undeniable."

He set his thermos back on the floor and leaned back in his chair. "Last night we all felt the power when you used it. It was like being on Olympus again." He looked up at the ceiling and smiled.

Danny set his backpack down. "Olympus? Isn't that where the Greek Gods live?" He sensed the hippie teacher had the answers he needed. "Who is Ty?"

"Typhon is the father of all monsters. He escaped from Tartarus sixteen years ago and waged war against the gods." He shook his head and sighed. "With help from the monsters, he destroyed Olympus and imprisoned Zeus and all the gods in Tartarus."

After last night, Danny believed all of this. But something didn't make sense. He had seen the man who called himself Ty, but nothing about him suggested he was capable of destroying gods.

"Before Olympus was destroyed, Zeus stripped all monsters of their powers," Mr. Silen continued like he could read Danny's mind. "They walk among us as humans now."

"Like you?" Danny remembered the image of horse legs and a tail on the hippie.

Mr. Silen nodded. "I am a teacher and companion to the gods."

"What does he want with me?"

He stood and looked into Danny's eyes. "Typhon wants to destroy this world and rebuild it as his own Olympus. Earthquakes, floods, tornados, hurricanes, famine. The rules have changed, and he can only do that in his true form as a monster. He must destroy the last descendant of Zeus before any of that can happen."

Danny laughed and ran his hands through his hair. "I don't know who you think I am, but I'm just a kid."

Mr. Silen stepped up to him and put a hand on his shoulder. "You were born for this, Alexandros. If you run into trouble, find Mr. Griffin."

Danny huffed. "The janitor?"

"He's so much more than that. Meet me after lunch. I have much to teach you."

Danny grabbed his backpack and headed for the door. He thought about calling his mom and getting a ride home. This was too much to handle. "I didn't choose any of this," he said as he unlocked the door.

"You were chosen by the gods. You are our last hope, Alexandros."

CHAPTER 11
SHAKESPEARE WASN'T AMERICAN

KEVIN SAT across from Danny at the same table in American History. He couldn't help but stare at Danny and try to figure out how to get him to trust him. He tried to prove his friendship by helping him outside, but Danny didn't fall for it at all. Danny was smart, but still pathetic.

"What are your thoughts on Shakespeare, Mr. Skinner?" Kevin looked toward the front of the room at Mr. Joyner. The teacher always wore a bowtie and had his hair greased back. He was young, maybe 20 years old, and always looked like he was on his way to his first prom. His mom probably still dressed him. How sad.

"He was the greatest writer of all time," Kevin said.

Mr. Joyner furrowed his eyebrows. "Care to expand on that?"

Kevin sighed. He didn't have time to waste on something so trivial. "He was a playwright, right? There are so many other forms of writing. I wonder if anyone would notice his work if he were alive today."

Bianca leaned across the table toward Kevin. She sat next to Danny and was tucked in close to him. "He also wrote sonnets and narrative poems."

"Good point, Miss Miller," the teacher said. "He wasn't a one hit wonder." Mr. Joyner chuckled to himself like a little girl, the way he always did when he thought he said something clever.

"Get away from me," Kevin hissed at Bianca. She thought she was so smart because she was a writer, too. The only thing she ever wrote were those stupid stories for the school newsletter.

"Anyone else care to weigh in?" Mr. Joyner asked.

Kevin chuckled and said, "Why are we even discussing this? I thought the name of this class was American History. Shakespeare was born and died in England."

Danny raised his hand. "It's because Shakespeare's work has been here as long as America has. He was widely read and his plays seen by Washington, Lincoln, and Adams."

"Kind of like the Beatles," Bianca said, slapping Danny on the back and laughing. She cleared her throat and looked up at Mr. Joyner with conviction in her eyes. "They had a lot more than one hit wonders, too."

The room burst out in laughter.

"Everyone calm down," Mr. Joyner said. "Now, Mr. Skinner, do you find anything unusual about Shakespeare's plays?"

"Other than the fact that they're boring?"

Mr. Joyner put a hand on his forehead. "Yes, other than that."

Kevin thought about it for a second. It didn't deserve any more time than that. He shrugged, crossed his arms, and leaned back.

Mr. Joyner straightened his bowtie like it somehow relieved tension. "How about you, Mr. Neumann?"

Danny tapped his fingers on the table then said, "Nothing unusual but he did use boys as female actors."

"Yes," the teacher said. "Can you tell me why?" He stood in front of Danny, leaned down, and placed a hand on the table.

Danny stared at the hand. Kevin thought he saw fear in Danny's eyes.

Becky raised her hand. "In Shakespeare's day it wasn't accepted for women to be actors."

Mr. Joyner stood back up and walked to the front of the class. "Thank you, Miss Miller. It wasn't a law, just society's acceptance at the time."

"So boys dressed up like girls?" Kevin said. He shivered like he was disgusted. "Cross-dressers scare me."

"Be that as it may," Mr. Joyner said, "it was what worked at the time. I find it rather interesting that anyone can disguise themselves to look like someone else completely."

The class bell rang and everyone gathered their books. Kevin sat and watched as Mr. Joyner stood in front of Danny again.

"Anyone can change the way they look, Danny," Mr. Joyner said. "They can wear different clothes, get a different haircut, or put on makeup. But don't forget that no one can hide the ugliness inside them."

Danny seemed to walk out of the room in a daze. Kevin couldn't make any sense out of it as he watched Mr. Joyner clean the dry erase board. Kevin stood and prepared to walk out. He laughed when he noticed a puny tattoo on the teacher's hand.

It was a blue oval, like a saucer.

CHAPTER 12
FROG LADY MAKES MEATLOAF

DANNY STARED ahead, eyes widened. A green monster waited for him at the front of the lunch line. It stood behind the cash register taking money and punching holes in lunch cards from starving teenagers. Its body was moist and covered in scales. Its eyes were narrow with yellow pupils that bulged out of its head.

"Do you see that?" Danny asked everyone around him.

Kevin stood next to him and looked ahead. "Ms. Lam? The lunch lady?"

Danny looked again at the green monster. "You don't see anything unusual about her?" As soon as he asked the question he knew the answer. He was the only one who could see and hear her as the monster she truly was.

Now he could see it was Ms. Lam. She was a nice old lady with wrinkles who always smiled at the kids.

Kevin shook his head and pushed Danny forward. "The only unusual thing I see is you, Freak."

Danny almost dropped his lunch tray full of meatloaf when he fell forward. He should have known better than to ask Kevin anything.

"$2.50," the green monster said when Danny stood in front of her. Danny thought he would be scared but the creature disgusted him. He reached into his jeans pocket, pulled out his lunch card and handed it to her.

Her eyes widened and her tongue shot out of her mouth like a frog's. Her tongue wrapped around the lunch card and pulled it back into her mouth. She chewed on it then spit it back out into Danny's face. He pulled the slimy mess off his forehead and stepped back, bumping into Kevin.

"No food for you, Danny Neumann," the monster hissed.

Kevin pushed him forward again. "Get off me, Freak."

Danny set his lunch tray on the counter and looked up at the monster. He had no idea how it knew his name. "Keep the food." He turned to walk away.

"Wait a minute," Kevin said. "Don't you want your lunch?"

Danny shook his head. "I don't have any money. It doesn't matter, though. I'm not hungry anymore."

Kevin stepped up to the monster who looked like a nice old lady again. "Ms. Lam, I'll pay for his lunch and mine." He nodded at Danny.

Danny couldn't believe what he was hearing. Kevin hadn't done anything nice all year. Maybe he wasn't such a bad guy after all. Maybe they were still best friends.

"You're such a good boy," the lunch lady said to Kevin.

Kevin balanced Danny's tray in one hand and his in the other, and stepped out of the line. "Here you go, buddy," he said to Danny, handing his tray to him.

Danny reached for it but Kevin pulled it away at the last second.

"Fat chance, Freak," Kevin said. "I'm really gonna enjoy eating your lunch." He laughed and walked away to the table of jocks. He turned when he got to the table and shouted back, "Maybe you should get a job! I'll pay you to wipe my ass!" The jocks laughed and high-fived him.

Danny took a deep breath and looked around the lunch room for a place to sit. The jocks were at one table and the cheerleaders next to them. The band and chorus had their own tables. Even the nerd table was full. There was only one table left with a few seats.

Danny stood next to William Sherman and asked if he could sit at the table. William was the only one there.

William looked up from his laptop and motioned for Danny to take a seat. Danny sat across the table from him and stared at him.

"Hey William," Danny said, "can I ask you something?"

William closed his laptop and studied Danny's face. "I don't know. Can you?"

Danny wasn't sure what he meant. "Huh?"

William sighed. "The proper way to ask such a question is, 'May I ask you something?'—not, 'Can I ask you something?'" He chuckled and rolled his eyes. "It's basic grammar, really."

Danny huffed. "You don't have many friends, do you?"

William's expression dropped. He opened his laptop back up and disappeared behind it.

Danny cracked his neck. "I'm sorry, William. You're the smartest guy I know, and I need your help."

William stuck his head up over his laptop.

"What do you see when you look at the lunch lady?" Danny asked.

William turned his head and looked at the green monster. "I see an elderly woman trapped in a lower middle class lifestyle serving crap to malnourished adolescents."

Danny's heart dropped. Aunt Ethel had gone to the nut house a few years ago. She saw things and people that no one else could.

"What do you see?" William asked.

Danny thought about it and decided he didn't have anything to lose by telling William. Nobody listened to him anyway. "I see a green monster."

William smirked. "That's why I don't read fiction."

Danny ignored him and looked down at the table. "She has scales over her body and yellow eyes. Her tongue comes out of her mouth like a frog's." He laughed at how it all sounded and looked back up at William. "Crazy, right?"

William looked at the green monster again. "Maybe not."

Danny sat up in his chair. "You believe me?"

William disappeared behind his laptop again. Danny could hear him typing. William looked up over his laptop and said, "Something like this?" He turned the laptop to face him.

Danny couldn't breathe. The laptop screen showed the image of the green monster. She did exist! "That's her!"

William turned the laptop back around. "This is not good." He typed furiously.

Danny jumped out of his seat and took the one next to William. "What is it?"

William stopped typing and stared ahead. "In fifth grade I did a paper on Greek mythology. It's nothing but fantasy fiction, circa 900 BC." He rested his hands on the table. "But some people believe it's all true."

"What is that thing?" Danny pointed at the green monster.

William looked at the monster again. "The person you're pointing at is Ms. Lam, which is an unusual coincidence because the creature in the picture I showed you is Lamia."

Danny cleared his throat. "Tell me about Lamia."

William turned to face him. His face lit up like he was excited to share his knowledge. "Lamia was a queen of Libya. Her beauty was unsurpassed." He looked over at the lunch lady and coughed. "The Greek god Zeus fell in love with her, and they had an affair. Zeus's wife Hera found out about it and killed her children."

Danny put his hands in the air. "That doesn't explain the green monster."

William put a finger over his lips. "This is the best part." He scooted in close. "Killing Lamia's children wasn't enough. Zeus's wife also turned Lamia into a monster that eats children."

Danny swallowed hard. He had not expected to hear this. If Lamia wanted to eat children, she was in the right place. This school had over a thousand students. But why would she be here centuries later?

William closed the laptop and sat back in his chair. "I'm not saying I believe any of it. It's all fantasy." He rubbed his chin. "If that's really Lamia over there..." He crossed his arms and looked straight up at the ceiling.

Danny shrugged. "What?"

"Then we're all in big trouble."

"SHE LOOKS like a frog," Danny said. "I'm going to call her Frog Lady."

William shook his head. "She's serpentine."

Danny stared across the room at the jocks' table. Becky was sitting next to Kevin now. Danny could hear Kevin burp from here. How in the world did Becky end up as Kevin's girlfriend?

"Maybe it's your destiny to save her," William whispered.

Danny had no idea what William was talking about. "How do I stop Frog Lady?"

"The more important question may be how would you kill her?" William put a hand on his chin. "Lamia would kill every kid here—if she really existed."

"No," Danny said. "That's not an option. There has to be another way."

William stretched his arms and yawned. "There may be another option. Lamia was cursed and unable to close her eyes. Zeus gave her the ability to remove her eyes so she could sleep." He laughed. "You could always steal her eyes."

"How?"

"It doesn't matter. If you're who I think you are, then you're destined to be a hero."

"Who's a hero?" Kevin asked as he walked up to them. "I don't see anything but losers at this table." He leaned across the table and put his face in front of Danny's. "I saw you looking at my girl. Do you have a death wish?"

"Leave them alone," Becky shouted from the other table.

Kevin smiled and turned around. "Be there in a second, babe. Just wishing my friend a belated happy birthday." He faced Danny again. "I hope you live to see your next birthday." He snatched William's thermos off the table and poured the soup from it into Danny's lap.

Danny jumped out of his seat and brushed as much soup off as he could. Everyone laughed at him. The band, chorus, jocks, cheerleaders, nerds—everyone. Danny stared as Becky ran out of the lunchroom and Kevin chased after her.

"He's just a stupid bully," Bianca Miller said, sliding into the seat next to Danny. She was a school reporter with a bouncy ponytail who never stopped talking. Everyone knew she had a crush on Danny.

"So, I'm writing a report on Meatloaf Mondays," she said.

Danny sighed and snatched some napkins from the nerd table. No one read the school newsletter. Even if they did, no one wanted to read about meatloaf.

"Ever since Ms. Lam started working here the meatloaf has been awesome," Bianca said. She giggled and smacked her lips. "She won't tell me the recipe, but I'm wearing her down."

"You should write about something more relevant to the world." William shook his head and continued typing.

Bianca crossed her arms. "Well, just so you know, Mr. Smarty Pants, I'm writing a story on the kids who have disappeared from school this year." She nodded like she was proud of herself.

William closed his laptop and looked at her. "It's because they're playing hooky. Which is fine with me because they'll be pumping my gas in a few years."

Danny couldn't help but think the two of them belonged together. Most of the soup was off his pants now. It would take a little longer for his jeans to dry out.

"How many kids have disappeared?" Danny realized there may be something to this story.

Bianca's face lit up. "Seven. I've asked the school administration about it, but they won't give me any answers."

"Maybe it's because you're annoying," William said.

She stuck her tongue out at him.

"How many Meatloaf Mondays have there been?" Danny asked.

Bianca looked at the table and counted silently with her lips. "Seven."

William pushed his lunch tray forward. "I'm done eating."

Danny stared at the lunch lady. He knew she looked innocent to everyone else, but if what William said earlier was true then she was a danger to everyone in this room. He couldn't help but think she had killed the seven missing kids and now was serving them for lunch.

"I've got to get into the back," Danny said to William and Bianca. He had to find out for sure if Frog Lady was killing the children and how to stop her.

"Why?" Bianca asked. "They won't even let me back there."

"Because he's going to save us," William said.

Danny nodded and looked at William. "Are you still on the debate team?"

"I'm the president."

Danny stood and stared at Frog Lady. "I'll help you get your story, Bianca." He turned and faced William again. "I need you to argue for our lives."

DANNY SAT at the lunch table with Bianca and watched as William went back into the lunch line. The plan had to work if they were going to get into the kitchen.

William handed Frog Lady his lunch card. Danny knew it had already been punched for today and expected Frog Lady to turn him away. Danny motioned for Bianca to stand up with him and go to the back of the line.

"No more food for you, William Sherman," he could hear Frog Lady say.

"My lunch card is still valid," William argued.

"You've already had your lunch," she responded, pointing to the hole punched in the card for today's date.

William adjusted his glasses. He stared at the card like he'd never seen it. "You're right, of course." He snatched the card from her and flipped it over. "Right here in the fine print it says we can only come through the line one time." He shook his head and cleared his throat. "Oh, wait. It doesn't say anything like that at all."

Frog lady scratched her head and closed her eyes. "No more food."

William stood there and stared at her. "I'm not getting out of this line without this food. Get me your supervisor."

"No supervisor."

William turned and faced the other two lunch ladies behind the counter. "Excuse me! Miss Lam doesn't know how to do her job. Can you ladies help me?" He was speaking loud enough for the entire lunchroom to hear.

Frog lady motioned for the ladies to join her.

William winked at Danny as the lunch ladies all came to the register. Danny was proud of him.

Danny grasped Bianca's wrist and stepped to the swivel door by the back of the line that gave entrance to the other side of the counter. He unlatched it and raced with Bianca to the kitchen in the back.

"What are we looking for?" Bianca asked. She was admiring the pots, pans, and even the sinks.

Danny scanned the room. "Evidence. But I don't think we'll find it in here." He looked at the walk in freezer. That's where meat would be kept.

"Come with me," Danny said. He opened the freezer door and noticed there wasn't a latch or lock on it. It was probably a safety protocol. He was glad for it. The thermostat said it was 0 degrees Fahrenheit inside.

After several minutes of searching through the containers and shelves Danny knew they wouldn't find anything. It was silly to think the lunch lady killed children and ate them. He should have never listened to William.

Danny motioned for Bianca to follow him and pressed on the freezer door to open it. It wouldn't budge. There was no knob or anything to turn. It was just a flat surface.

"Let me open it," Bianca said. She pushed Danny aside and pressed on the door. It still didn't move. "Help!"

Danny stared at the temperature gage inside the freezer. It said -25 degrees Fahrenheit. His heart stopped when he realized someone had blocked them inside and turned the temperature all the way down.

CHAPTER 13
TURNING DOWN THE THERMOSTAT

KEVIN GRASPED Becky's arm and turned her around. Who the hell did she think she was running away from him?

"You're hurting me," she whined.

Kevin didn't know why but he was breathing hard and his heart was racing. "This is because of Danny." He threw her arm back and pounded his fists together. "I won't let him get in my way."

Becky pushed him. She was so weak. Kevin felt sorry for her. She would never admit it, but any idiot could see she was in love with Danny. Why would she want a loser like Danny over him?

"This has nothing to do with Danny," Becky pouted. "It has everything to do with you." She crossed her arms and bit her lower lip. "This isn't working."

Kevin pulled her into the hall away from everyone and shoved her against the wall. She had no right to end things with him. He was the man, damn it!

Becky's face was red, and she gasped for air. Kevin stepped back. He didn't realize he was holding her neck. "I'm sorry," he said with his hands up. "I would never hurt you."

Becky coughed and walked further down the hall. "Don't ever touch me again. We're through!" Her shoulders shuddered and her sniffles echoed in the empty hallway.

Every muscle in Kevin's body tensed. She couldn't talk to him like that! "Keep walking!"

Kevin paced the hallway and tried to catch his breath. He needed to hit something. The energy inside of him was screaming to get free.

"Danny has to pay."

He looked into the lunchroom at Danny's table, but it was empty. Where the hell was Danny at? He heard someone at the front of the lunch line screaming about wanting to speak with a supervisor. It was William Sherman. That kid was such a geek.

He followed William's gaze and saw him wink at Danny at the end of the lunch line. Danny grabbed some tramp and took her into the kitchen. He was probably going to make out with her.

Kevin marched back into the cafeteria and headed for the kitchen. All of the lunch ladies were too busy arguing with William to notice him.

He searched around the kitchen, but Danny and his tramp were nowhere to be found. Right before he gave up he heard mumbled voices from the freezer. That was an interesting place to make out—he'd have to remember it.

Kevin looked at the thermostat and saw it was at 0 degrees Fahrenheit. "Not cold enough." He turned it all the way down. He reached for the nearest oven and pushed it with one hand in front of the freezer door. He seized a second oven and sat it next to the first one. Then he hoisted a refrigerator over his head and stacked it sideways on top of the ovens. A pathetic loser like Danny wasn't strong enough to move that.

Someone inside screamed, "Help!"

Kevin laughed and leaned back against the ovens. The two of them wouldn't be screaming anything pretty soon. He had no idea how long it took to freeze to death, but now was as good a time as any to find out. Lunch hour would be over in about twenty minutes.

Kevin yawned and thought about the old man. Whoever the guy was he gave him these awesome powers. Now he was stronger than everyone else. No steroids needed. And the old fart said he'd get everything he wanted when Danny died. It seemed horrible and something he would never do at first. But this wasn't so bad. He didn't have to see Danny die. He was doing Danny a favor.

Kevin tried to think about everything he ever wanted. This power was at the top of the list, but something else kept popping into his head. He wanted Becky back, and he'd do whatever it took to get her.

Becky was boring and predictable. She was probably an eight on a scale of one – ten. Not too bad but he could do a lot better. She was lucky to have someone like him in her life. He could make her world so much better.

Kevin felt someone press against the freezer door. They were so weak. His body didn't even move.

Fifteen more minutes of lunch. If they weren't frozen popsicles by then he'd have to go in and rip their heads off their bodies.

CHAPTER 14
REVEALING THE ENEMY

DANNY STOOD over Bianca and rubbed her shoulders. She was sitting on the freezer floor, shivering, rocking back and forth. Danny didn't feel anything at all. He realized he couldn't sense the cold.

"How...are...you...still...standing?" Bianca sounded like she could barely breathe. Every sound she made was labored.

"I'm used to the cold," Danny lied. He had grown up in South Florida and hated cold weather. His parents took him to the North Carolina Mountains one winter, and he had never been so miserable. He looked at his arms and was amazed he didn't even have goose bumps.

Bianca wiped her nose with her shirt sleeve. Her normally bouncy ponytail was pointed straight down. "We're...in...trouble," she said. She was right. If they didn't get out of here soon then Bianca would go into some kind of shock, he was sure.

Danny pushed on the freezer door again as hard as he could. It wouldn't move. He tried to think how it was possible because he knew there was no lock on it and he was supposed to be strong like a god. There was only one explanation. Someone had trapped them in here.

Danny heard Bianca's body thump on the floor. She lay there and shivered uncontrollably. Her lips were blue. "No, no, no, no, no!" He ripped his shirt off and covered her torso with it. He lifted her lifeless body, and hoisted her over his shoulder effortlessly.

"Stay with me. We're getting out of here."

Danny stared at the door and focused on how he had pushed Ty back. He threw his arms toward the door and grunted. Nothing happened. He closed his eyes and took a deep breath. Bianca's breathing was faint, and her heart beat slowly. He had to get her out now!

Danny felt his body tense with an energy that had to be released from it. A familiar tingling sensation started from the balls of his feet, rose through his torso, and burned in his arms and hands. His eyes shot open, and he threw his arms forward again.

A ball of energy shot out from his hands and blew the door off its hinges. It flew across the room and bounced off the opposite wall, where it crumpled to the floor bent in half. Two ovens and a refrigerator were scattered in different parts of the kitchen.

Danny couldn't move. Not because of what he had done. But because of who he saw standing outside the door.

"Kevin," he whispered.

"Get out of there!" Kevin yelled. He was waving his hands for Danny to come toward him. "I heard someone shout for help."

Danny raced out and set Bianca on the floor. Her chest rose and fell, and she shivered again. He ran to the remaining ovens, turned them all the way up and opened the doors. He ran back to Bianca, sat behind her, pulled her toward him, and wrapped her body in his arms.

"It's going to be okay," he whispered to her. "I'm here for you."

"Thank god you're okay," Kevin said. "What happened?"

Danny looked up at Kevin. He knew Kevin had something to do with this, but he had no idea why. Had Kevin been holding the door? If he had, how could he be stronger than him?

"What the hell is going on in here?" Ms. Spin stepped into the room and stared at the bent door. "And why is your shirt off?" She was the In School Suspension teacher and no one liked her. She always dressed in a pantsuit and had a boy's haircut.

Danny didn't say anything. Kevin didn't either. Bianca opened her eyes. Her body was warm. Her ponytail was bouncy again.

Danny felt weak and exhausted. Somehow he knew some of his energy had transferred to Bianca.

Frog Lady walked in next to Ms. Spin and said, "Oh, my. I hope the children are okay."

"You and you, head to the ISS room," Ms. Spin ordered Danny and Kevin. "You," she pointed to Bianca, "stay here and help Ms. Lam clean up this mess. I don't know how you got mixed up with these hooligans."

"She should see the nurse," Danny said. He retrieved his shirt from Bianca and put it back on. He knew Bianca was okay now, but he couldn't leave her with Ms. Lam. There still wasn't any evidence to know if she had been killing children or not.

"She looks fine to me," Ms. Spin said. "ISS room. Now." She pointed toward the cafeteria.

"Find me if you need me," Danny whispered to Bianca. "Run if you have to."

"I'll be okay," Bianca said. She stared at her hands like she had never seen them before. "I've never felt better."

Danny walked toward the exit.

"I'm so glad you can stay," Danny heard Ms. Lam tell Bianca. "We can have meatloaf again tomorrow."

CHAPTER 15
SUGAR AND SPICE

BIANCA WATCHED Danny walk out of the kitchen. He was so cute! His dark blue eyes and broad shoulders always made her heart skip a beat. Why hadn't he asked her out yet? No matter. She'd write him a poem one day, and he'd be hers forever!

"Start cleaning," Ms. Lam said. She was bossy for an old lady. She didn't seem to like kids at all, and Bianca had no idea why she worked here. She was so old she walked with her back hunched over and a limp.

Bianca picked up a white knob from the floor. It looked the piece from one of the ovens that turned the temperature up or down. "Where does this go?"

Ms. Lam limped over to her and snatched the knob. "Where does this go?" she mocked in a high voice then slapped it on a small metal bar on the closest oven. Bianca knew her voice didn't sound like that. She had recorded her voice many times in interviews. Speaking of interviews…

"So, Ms. Lam, it looks like this will take awhile." Bianca snatched a notepad from her back pocket. It had a small pencil in the metal spirals on top. "Let's talk about your famous meatloaf. How do you make it?"

Ms. Lam huffed. "You don't give up—do you, girlie?"

Bianca smiled and shook her head. Persistent—that's what everyone said she was. Her parents said she leaned to walk at seven months old, ahead of all her cousins. Why? Because every time she stood and fell down she jumped right back up. It didn't matter how many times she fell. She had refused to crawl anymore.

"Push that oven back against the wall," Ms. Lam said, pointing at the oven that had all its knobs back now.

Bianca looked at it and laughed. It was way too heavy for her to move unless it had wheels. She put her hands on it. "Here goes nothing."

"Sometimes I use snips and snails to make my meatloaf," Ms. Lam said from behind her.

The oven escaped from Bianca's hands and banged against the wall on the other side of the room. She held her palms in front of her face. How was this possible?

"Other times," Ms. Lam said, standing behind Bianca and breathing heavily on her ponytail, "I use sugar and spice."

Bianca turned to find Ms. Lam facing her with some kind of butcher knife. Ms. Lam contorted her face, raised the knife, and thrust it toward Bianca's head.

Bianca froze. She had been right about the meatloaf, and Ms. Lam's old wrinkly face was the last thing she'd ever see. She wasn't supposed to die like this. She was supposed to win the Pulitzer one day or at least write a feature article for the Sunday newspaper.

The knife never touched Bianca's head. She blocked Ms. Lam's arm and shoved her hands against Ms. Lam's stomach. She watched Ms. Lam fly toward the wall the same way the oven had.

Ms. Lam crashed into the wall then fell face down. She didn't move anymore.

Bianca stared at her palms again. "This is awesome!"

CHAPTER 16
MS. SPIN AND THE BROKEN DESK

DANNY HAD never been inside the ISS room, but it looked like every other classroom in this school. There were twenty-five – thirty desks lined up in rows with enough space to walk between them horizontally. They all faced the dusty chalkboard behind the teacher's desk. "Home away from home."

Danny couldn't hide his shock when he saw Becky sitting at one of the front desks. His mouth fell open. "What are you doing here?" he whispered as he walked by. He took a seat next to her.

Kevin took the seat on the other side of Becky. "Back off," he said, leaning across the desk and staring at Danny.

Ms. Spin stood in front of them and shook her head. "I have two rules in this room." She held up her index finger. "Number One — don't kill each other." She raised her middle finger next to her index finger. "Number Two — keep your mouths closed."

Danny couldn't take his eyes off her. He could see she had the body of a lion and wings like an eagle. He wished William was here to tell him what she was.

Ms. Spin walked back to the class door. "There's one more person to add to this party," she said. "Don't miss me too much." And then she was gone.

"Okay," Becky said. "That was rude."

Danny turned in his seat to face Becky. "Why are you here? Are you okay?"

She swiveled to meet him and hunched over. Their mouths almost touched. "I was walking in the halls, thinking about things." She paused and took a deep breath. "I want things to be different."

Danny wanted to hear what she had to say but couldn't stop staring at her neck. It had a red ring around it. "How did you get that?"

Kevin stood in front of Danny's desk. "Mind your own business or I'm gonna have to break Ms. Spin's first rule." He pounded his fist on the wooden desk and the front shelf broke in half.

The class door opened and Ms. Spin walked in with William. "Sit down and shut up," she screamed at Kevin. She motioned for William to take a seat. He sat in the back.

Danny got up to sit next to William.

"Where do you think you're going?" Ms Spin asked.

Danny pointed to his seat. "My desk is broken."

Ms. Spin sat behind her desk and folded her hands. "Whatever." She took a magazine off her desk and started reading it. "Deviants," everyone could hear her say from behind the magazine.

"Hey," Danny whispered as he slid into a seat next to William. "I need to ask you something."

"You're welcome," William whispered back.

"What?"

"For getting you into the kitchen. Now I have a blemish on my school record. Goodbye Harvard."

Danny scrunched his lips. He didn't mean to get William in trouble. "I'm sorry. But listen…remember how I told you Ms. Lam looks like a frog?"

William nodded. He sighed like he knew trouble was coming.

"What kind of creature has a body like a lion and wings like an eagle?"

William put a hand under his chin. "What does its face look like?"

Danny looked back up as Ms. Spin. She put her magazine down to see if anyone was talking or killing someone else. Satisfied she buried her face back in the magazine.

"It looks like Ms. Spin," Danny said.

William leaned back and chuckled. "Of course. It makes too much sense." He stopped laughing when Danny frowned at him. "You described the Sphinx from Greek mythology. But that's impossible. She's already dead."

Danny raised his eyebrows. "Not if she escaped from Tartarus like Ty did. Tell me about the Sphinx."

William leaned forward. "The Sphinx guarded a city's entrance and asked a riddle to any traveler who tried to enter." He cracked his neck. "Anyone who couldn't answer the riddle, well—"

"Excuse me, gentlemen," Ms. Spin said, standing over them. "I believe you broke rule number two." She held up her two fingers for emphasis. "Sit back and shut up!"

Danny sat back and watched Ms. Spin walk back up front. She stopped at her desk and sat on the front of it, facing Becky.

"I have a riddle for you, Miss Goody Two-shoes," Ms. Spin said to Becky.

Danny turned back to William and whispered, "What happens if she can't answer?"

William held up a hand for Danny to be silent.

"If you can answer the riddle," Ms. Spin continued, "I'll let everyone in this room go back to class and continue living their miserable lives."

"William," Danny whispered harshly. "What if she can't answer it?"

Danny felt a whoosh, and he saw Ms. Spin as the Sphinx again. "If she answers incorrectly, then I'm going to kill your friends and eat them!"

Danny couldn't breathe. He was glad no one else could see or hear her as the monster she was. "Let me answer it."

The Sphinx laughed. "The rules have changed, Alexandros Helen. Besides, you weren't the one wandering the halls." She laughed and put her face in front of his. "I can't touch you. But I sure as hell can rip your friends apart."

Danny's body tensed. The energy was building up inside him again. He was prepared to use his power if needed. The Sphinx couldn't touch him, but he wouldn't hesitate to hurt her to protect his friends.

Becky shrugged and said, "Ask me the question."

Ms. Spin leaned forward from her position on the desk. "Today's category is transportation. What can you always find in cars, boats, and planes but never find in trucks, ships, or helicopters?"

Becky folded her hands and rested her chin on them. It's what she always did when she didn't know something and was thinking hard about it.

"The next class bell rings in three minutes," Ms. Spin said. "You must answer before then." She smirked and picked her magazine back up.

William rubbed his forehead. Danny looked at him and held his hands up.

"I know the answer," William whispered.

Becky still had her hands under her chin.

"Write it down in large letters," Danny whispered, pointing at the notepad on William's desk.

"What? Why?"

"Just do it." Danny motioned for William to give him a piece of paper, too. He took the sheet and broke off small tabs. He sucked on the tabs and formed them into balls.

"Really?" William said. "Spitballs? You know they're too far away for that."

Danny waved him off. "Do you have the answer written down?"

William nodded.

Danny picked up one of the spitballs and threw it at the back off Becky's head. It bounced off her thick hair. When she didn't even move, he frowned.

"Dang," William said. "You've got a great arm. You should play baseball."

Ms. Spin lay her magazine down. "There's one minute left. Do you have the answer, Miss Goody Two-shoes?"

"Not yet," Becky said.

Ms. Spin looked back at Danny and winked. She picked her magazine back up. Danny could hear her laughing from behind it.

There wasn't much time left before his friends would be dead. Danny took the next spitball and tossed it at Kevin. It hit the back of his head. He swatted at it like he thought it was a fly.

Danny had three spitballs left. He picked them all up and threw them at once at Kevin. One hit his left ear, one hit his neck, and the other bounced off his head.

Kevin jumped out of his seat and glared at Danny.

"Sit down," Ms. Spin said.

Kevin slid back in his seat but turned around. His nose flared.

Ms. Spin buried her head behind the magazine and mumbled some nonsense.

William held up the paper he had written on. He waved at Kevin and pointed at the paper.

Kevin shrugged like he was confused.

Danny pointed at the paper then at Becky. He went back and forth three times before Kevin seemed to finally understand.

Kevin turned to Becky and shook her shoulder. He mouthed just one syllable when Becky looked at him.

"Twenty seconds, little lady," Ms. Spin said. "Tick tock, tick tock."

Becky lowered her arms for the first time. "I have the answer."

Danny looked at the clock and saw there were ten seconds left.

"A," Becky said. "You can find the letter 'A' is in cars, boats, and planes but not in trucks, ships, or helicopters."

The class bell rang.

Ms. Spin put her magazine down and put her hands over her head. "Go on to class. Get out of here. All of you."

Danny stood and gave William a high five. Becky looked back at him and smiled. Danny walked up to her desk and looked over at Kevin. "Thank you. We couldn't have done this without you."

"Go to hell." Kevin stood and walked out of the room.

"Your boyfriend's hard to please," Danny said to Becky, shaking his head.

"We're taking a break. I need to think about things."

Danny pointed to Becky's neck. "Did he have something to do with this?"

Becky headed for the door. "It doesn't matter. I need a friend right now, Danny Neumann. I need you."

CHAPTER 17
SNAKE LADY WEARS A SHORT DRESS

DANNY WALKED into the hallway with Becky. She leaned against his side and rested her head on his shoulder.

"I didn't choose you because I don't ever want to lose our friendship," she said.

He put an arm around her side. He didn't agree with her, but maybe it was for the best. He had a new life now and couldn't put hers in danger.

She stopped and grabbed his hands. "You're the best thing that's ever happened to me."

"Get a room," William said when he passed them.

"We have to get to class," Becky said. "Meet me after school at the Fall Festival?"

Danny nodded. His heart skipped a few beats.

She squeezed his hands and walked to her next class.

Danny stood there a moment and felt the energy surge through his body. Only this time he didn't want to release it. He wanted to hold onto it forever.

"Danny Neumann to Vice Principle Echid's office," the speakers in the hallway squeaked. "Danny Neumann to Vice Principle Echid's office."

Danny looked at his watch. He was supposed to meet Mr. Silen for some kind of training and answers. It looked like it would have to wait.

He went to the front office and took a seat by Ms. Echid's door. He knew he was here because of the damage in the kitchen. He had no idea how to explain why the door bent in half.

Ms. Echid's door opened, and she motioned for him to come in. She was the most beautiful woman he had ever seen with her large blue eyes and long eyelashes. She was probably about thirty-five years old, but could pass for twenty. She always wore a short dress and perfume that made you want to get closer to her.

Danny sat down across from her desk. "I can pay for the damages."

Ms. Echid closed the door. "That's not why you're here." She twisted the blinds closed.

Danny swallowed hard for some reason. He was alone in this room with a beautiful woman. He saw on the news just last week where a pretty young female teacher went to prison for fooling around with a student like him.

She traced her hands over his back then sat down at her desk. "I heard you're having an interesting day."

Danny had no intention of telling her anything. He didn't expect anyone to believe what he'd experienced so far today. "The best thing about my day has been the meatloaf."

Ms. Echid laughed. "The meatloaf here is really good. Makes you wonder what the ingredients are."

Danny nodded. "Other than that, everything here is great."

The office phone rang, and Ms. Echid held up a finger. "Yes?" she said into the receiver. "Oh, god." She leaned forward. "Paramedics are on the way? Good. Keep me apprised." She set the receiver down and stared at Danny.

"Is everything okay?"

Ms. Echid shook her head. "You've been a naughty boy, Alexandros Helen."

Danny sat up straight. He had no idea how he had missed it. He was blinded by her beauty. Her lower body looked like a snake's. "Who are you?"

She stood and leaned across the desk. "I'm an angry mother whose children are in danger. And I will do anything to protect them." She rounded the desk and put her hands on Danny's shoulders. "And you need to know the truth."

Danny squirmed. He wasn't comfortable with Snake Lady touching him. "What truth?"

She let go of his shoulders and stood back. "I know you've spoken with Mr. Silen. I'm sure he's filled your head with nonsense. I should have fired that drunkard years ago."

Danny didn't want to listen to her, but it didn't look like he had much of a choice. At least his friends were safe this time. He could fend for himself.

"Did he tell you how your parents died?" Snake Lady asked.

Danny didn't answer. He wasn't comfortable discussing his dead parents with a snake. His throat constricted as if he was suffocating.

"He probably told you they were struck by some random flash of lightning." Ms. Echid laughed. "It wasn't random, Alexandros. Zeus controls the skies and thunderbolts." She stared into his eyes. "Zeus killed your parents."

Danny couldn't move. He didn't believe what Snake Lady said, but it made sense for some reason.

"If you don't believe me, ask Mr. Silen yourself." She shook her head and went back to her seat. Her lips drooped like she was sad for Danny. "Sometimes the truth hurts, Alexandros. I don't know why he killed them. We're just lucky that you were born."

Danny cleared his throat. "Is that why he's in Tartarus?"

"Yes."

Danny didn't believe Snake Lady but all of this was confusing. He had to get out of here and talk to Mr. Silen.

"You were never supposed to be born, Alexandros. You were a mistake."

DANNY STEPPED out of the office in a daze. Was he really a mistake who was never meant to be born? He had to speak with Mr. Silen.

He stopped as paramedics raced past him in the hallway. Several teachers and students stood in the hall.

"What's happening?" Danny asked the one face he recognized. He couldn't forget the spiked hair and makeup.

Becky's friend Marc put a hand over his chest. "Ms. Spin tried to kill herself. She slit her wrists. How horrible."

Danny nodded. *Good.*

"I heard the news, Lover Boy." Marc put his hand up for a high five. "Now's your chance to get the girl."

Danny ignored the hand and continued to Mr. Silen's room. Marc huffed behind him and slapped his own hand.

"Danny, I'm glad you made it," Mr. Silen said as he walked in. "We have a lot to talk about, and I'll show you a few tricks. Have a seat."

Danny stood there and said, "Did Zeus kill my parents?"

Mr. Silen sat at his desk and pulled his thermos to his mouth. "It's not that simple."

"Yes it is. Did he kill my parents? Yes or no?"

"Yes, but—"

Danny held out a hand. "We don't have anything else to talk about." Danny ran out of the room and nearly knocked Becky over.

"Danny, wait," she said. "What's going on?"

"I'm late for class," Danny lied. "See you tonight." He turned and walked toward the gym.

"BECKY, COME in here for a minute please," Mr. Silen said.

She watched Danny disappear down the hall. "Always running away from something," she whispered.

"How are you today?" Mr. Silen asked when she stepped into the room. Becky always liked Mr. Silen. He had a great outlook on life and didn't seem to care what anyone else thought. He was teacher of the year at this school five years in a row. All the kids liked him and they all got good grades. It wasn't a matter of Mr. Silen just passing everyone. They all scored really high on the state tests thanks to him.

"I'm great. And you?"

"Can't complain," Mr. Silen said. "I wanted to talk to you about Danny."

Becky didn't know what this was about, but Danny could be in trouble for something. He seemed different today after the news he got last night. She knew he was just hurting. She wanted to be with him right now.

"He's going through a rough time," Becky said. "But I know Danny, and he'll work through it."

"That's what I'm counting on." Mr. Silen leaned back in his desk chair. "He won't listen to me. He needs someone to believe in him."

Becky huffed. "I believe in him."

Mr. Silen got up and closed the door. He took his hippie glasses off and said, "Good. There's something we need to talk about."

CHAPTER 18
ARE WE BOYS OR ARE WE MEN?

DANNY SAT on a bench in the locker room and changed into his gym shorts. He didn't feel the energy inside him anymore. It was like it flew away when he found out he was never meant to be born. Some god he was.

"You been working out, dude?" The guy behind him was hovering over him.

Danny shook his head. He never lifted weights.

"You're getting buff, dude. Keep it up." The guy walked out.

Danny opened his locker and looked in the mirror on the door. He didn't recognize himself. His chest felt like boulders when he touched it. His abs were sculpted into a six pack. Wait, they looked like an eight pack. He flexed his arms and watched his biceps inflate like tires. "This is impossible."

He could see someone else's reflection right behind him. Danny turned and was looking right into Kevin's eyes.

"Anything's possible," Kevin said. His eyes seemed empty, and his expression was blank. His body was built exactly like Danny's.

How did either of them end up like this? Danny realized that somehow Kevin had the same powers as him. But how did he get them? Danny was the last descendant.

"May the best man win," Kevin said as he strode out of the gym.

Danny put his gym shirt on and tried to figure out what Kevin meant. He imagined he meant the best man for Becky.

"Life is funny sometimes, isn't it, young lad?" Danny turned to see the janitor Mr. Griffin mopping the floors. He was a black man who always walked with his back slightly bent.

"What?"

"You expect the train of life to go one way, but before you know it, you're jumping off the tracks in some city you've never heard of." He stopped and wiped the sweat from his forehead. "And you hope nobody robs you."

Danny shoved his clothes into his locker and shut it. The janitor sounded like he'd been sniffing too many chemicals.

"Has anybody robbed you, Alexandros Helen?"

Danny tightened his fists. He couldn't face anymore monsters today. He didn't feel the power in his body. It was like he had been... robbed. He turned and faced the janitor to see his true form.

Danny couldn't breathe. Mr. Griffin was a massive beast with the body of a lion and wings like an eagle. Even his head looked like an eagle. He was magnificent to look at.

"What are you?" Danny said.

"A friend. Everyone needs a friend when they've lost their way."

"How did you know?"

"I've been your guardian since they day you were born."

Danny didn't know how to feel about this. Was this man a stalker? Or someone sent by the gods to protect him?

Mr. Griffin looked like a janitor again. He smiled and set his mop against a locker. "Time for a break." He set a lunch pail on the bench. "Want half of a peanut butter sandwich?"

Danny shook his head. He wasn't sure how to talk to this man. He wasn't sure how to talk to anyone anymore.

"I know you have questions about your parents," Mr. Griffin said. He bit into his sandwich and chewed on it. "This is really good. I love the way the peanut butter sticks to the top of my mouth."

Danny cleared his throat. "My parents?"

Mr. Griffin winked at him and nodded. "I was your father's guardian, too." He took another bite and then a swig from his soda can. "I was there the day he and your mom died."

Danny leaned against his locker. "What happened that day?"

Mr. Griffin set his sandwich down. "Now I have your attention, young lad." He stretched his legs out and crossed them at the same time he crossed his arms. "Typhon wants control of the Earth. He has to kill the demigods to do that."

Danny sat on the bench next to him. "There's more like me?"

Mr. Griffin shook his head. "Not anymore. Typhon sent his army of monsters to wipe the demigods out." He stopped and looked down. "We fought them as long as we could. But they were too powerful."

"And my parents?"

"I'm getting to that, young lad." He laughed and slapped Danny on the back. "Your parents were the last demigods left. Typhon wanted to execute them himself. He needed proof they had no descendants."

Danny scratched his arm. "I don't understand. What about the other demigods?"

Mr. Griffin laughed. "They were all important, but none of them were married to each other. Your father was the son of Apollo. Your mother, the daughter of Harmonia." He sighed and smiled. "You're the first offspring of two demigods. No one knows what you're capable of."

Danny listened as the janitor recounted everything that happened the day he was born. His parents prayed to Zeus to take their lives but to spare his. It was the only way to save him. They knew the monsters would kill them and rip their bodies to shreds. That's when Zeus struck them with lightning and formed a protective shield around Danny.

"Your parents made preparations for that day," Mr. Griffin continued. "They loved you very much. They made sure you would be raised by a loving family. It was their hope that the monsters would never find out you existed."

"How did they find me?"

"For sixteen years they've all sensed there was someone or something magical in this city. Your power is strong, Alexandros. It was only a matter of time."

Danny stood and stretched his arms. "How many like you are there?"

Mr. Griffin sighed. "I'm the only one. The others are all in Tartarus with the gods. Maybe one day we'll get them out together." He walked back over to his mop. "But not today. I've got a sweaty gym to clean up."

"What is my purpose?

Mr. Griffin leaned against his mop. "Your purpose is the same as everyone else's. Hop back on the train of life and stay on it until you get to where you were supposed to go all along." He smiled and whistled as he disappeared with his mop behind a group of lockers.

DANNY WENT into the gym and sat with his peers on the bleachers. This was his least favorite part of the day. He was never good at any sports, and the only sit-up he did was when he got out of bed.

"Today we're going to play dodge ball, ladies," Coach Spradley said. He was a short guy who always talked loudly and made everyone feel inferior. He wore biker shorts and a wife-beater. He didn't look like a monster, but Danny really didn't like him right now.

"He suffers from an Oedipus complex," someone whispered to him.

Danny turned to see William sitting next to him. He couldn't help but smile. It was the strangest thing because before today, Danny would have never considered William his friend. But now William felt like his best friend. It was good to have a best friend again.

"Are you skipping class?" Danny knew William was supposed to be in Calculus or Chemistry or some kind of class that smart people went to.

"You already got me kicked out of Harvard. I figured I'd come here and let you ruin the rest of my life." He spoke in his usual monotone voice but smirked.

Danny punched him in the arm. "You believed me."

"Ow."

"Sorry."

Danny told William about what happened with Ms. Echid. He mentioned how she was so beautiful he hadn't noticed at first she was part snake. He didn't mention how she said he was a mistake.

"It all makes sense," William said. He rubbed a hand on his chin and grimaced. "I think we're in real trouble. Echidna is the mother of all monsters."

"KEVIN AND Mike will be team captains," Coach Spradley said.

Danny already knew which team he wouldn't be on. He waited as Kevin and Mike selected their teams. He was the last person selected on Mike's team. He didn't care, but it was always embarrassing.

William left after Danny told him about everything that happened since last night. He seemed fascinated and helped Danny make some sense of what was happening.

There was nothing to worry about.

Danny squirmed in the hard bleacher seat. He was selected as an alternate for Mike's team and forced to sit here unless called in. He looked at the two teams standing across from each other in horizontal lines. There were eight teenagers on both sides. Six balls waited on the attack line between them.

Mr. Spradley blew his whistle and everyone raced to snatch a ball. Kevin was the first one there. He grabbed a ball and threw it in the face of some skinny kid right in front of him. The kid crashed on the floor.

Kevin caught the ball when it bounced off his face, and threw it into the gut of Big Tommy. Big Tommy weighed three hundred pounds. Kevin laughed and looked into the bleachers at Danny. He put his fists together then pulled them apart at an angle, like he was breaking bread.

Danny watched as Kevin took out kid after kid. He was a one man show. It wasn't long before twenty-seven minutes had passed, and three rounds were over. Kevin's team had won one round, and Mike's team had won two. Kevin's team would have won them all if he had worked with his teammates. Mr. Spradley had said they were playing five rounds if needed to declare a winner.

They were in the fourth round when Danny heard a familiar voice. "You used to tell me everything, Danny Neumann."

Becky stood by the bleachers next to him. She stared at the game on the court. He didn't know what to say to her. He couldn't explain what happened with Mr. Silen or tell her the truth about himself. And even if he could, how could she ever love him?

"I'm sorry, Becky. I understand if you never want to talk to me again."

"I know everything," she said. She clutched his shirt collar and pulled him toward her. "I can handle it." Her breath was warm against his face.

"Skinner!" coach Spradley shouted.

Danny looked back at the court. Kevin marched toward them. He did not look happy. Balls flew all around him. Kevin stopped and looked at the two of them. He clenched his jaw and shook his head.

Danny saw a ball sailing straight for Kevin's head. *Good.*

Kevin never turned to face the ball. He reached out and caught it with one hand. It was so sudden that no one made a sound.

Then Kevin's teammates cheered him on and patted him on the back. . The game was 2 - 2 now.

Big Tommy hobbled to the bleachers. He sat on the first row in front of Danny. "I knew I shouldn't have eaten those jelly donuts." The armpits on his shirt were drenched in sweat. "Coach wants you on the court."

Danny looked back at the court to see Kevin standing there with his arms crossed.

"Go get him, Danny," Becky said.

Danny nodded and stepped out of the bleachers. He went to the team captain Mike. The team was gathered around him in a huddle.

"Okay, guys," Mike said, "this is our last chance. Are we boys or are we men?"

"Men!" they all shouted.

"I can't hear you! Are we boys or are we men?"

"Men!"

Debbie held up a hand. She was the only girl on the team. "Uh, I'm not a man. Gross."

Coach Spradley blew his whistle, and they all lined up. Danny focused on the ball on the attack line he planned to get. His only objective was to take Kevin out. When he looked up, he saw that Kevin was staring at the ball right next to his.

Coach Spradley blew his whistle again. Danny raced for the attack line. He was ahead of everyone else. Kevin was ahead of his team, too. Danny reached his ball at the same time Kevin reached the one next to it. They both snatched a ball with one hand and pounded them toward each other.

The balls slammed together and exploded. Danny and Kevin both fell to the floor. Everyone stopped and stared at them.

"So we have crappy balls," Coach Spradley said. "Keep playing!"

Balls flew all around Danny. He jumped back up and avoided them. He was amazed how limber and flexible he was. It was like nothing could touch him. He caught a ball and threw it at Kevin.

Kevin grabbed the kid next to him and shoved him in front of him. It bounced off his head. The kid walked off the court in a daze.

Danny stopped and looked around. No balls were flying. No one was left on the court except him and Kevin. Danny collected two balls and threw them back to back like missiles at Kevin.

Kevin fell to his back then jumped up like a ninja as soon as the balls passed. "You're gonna have to do better than that." He lobbed four balls in a row at Danny.

Danny jumped and twisted and turned. His body moved in a fluid motion in every direction. The balls didn't touch him.

"Thirty seconds, ladies," Coach Spradley said.

Danny stared at Kevin. Kevin stared back at him. "Make your move."

"Get him, Danny!" Becky shouted from the bleachers.

Kevin turned when she said that, and Danny knew it was his chance. His muscles tightened as the energy built up inside him. He picked up a ball and shot it toward Kevin with his energy behind it.

Kevin turned and shouted, "NO!" right as the ball slammed into his gut. He seemed to slide a few feet back before crashing to the floor.

Danny's team roared and ran up to him with high fives and congratulations.

"What are we?" Mike shouted.

"Men!"

Debbie shook her head. "I give up."

DANNY LOOKED into the bleachers to give a thumbs-up to Becky. He was relieved to know that she accepted him for who he was. She was the source of his energy. She was the essence of his passion.

Danny never put his thumb up. Standing next to Becky were Snake Lady and Frog Lady. They looked pissed. Snake Lady clapped her hands in slow motion. She looked from Danny to Becky, making the connection that he liked her.

Danny took a wide stance when Snake Lady and Frog Lady hissed and came toward him. He didn't think they'd attack him in public. Surely they knew he was more powerful than they were. Did the Sphinx die and they wanted retribution? It was possible. William said the Sphinx was Echidna's daughter.

Danny heard a loud whistling from the locker room. Mr. Griffin walked out with his mop bucket in tow. He winked at Danny as his image transformed into the magnificent lion with wings and an eagle's head. He roared at the monsters. The whole gym shook.

Snake Lady and Frog Lady stopped and took two steps back. Then they turned and ran out of the gym.

Mr. Griffin looked like a janitor again. He nodded at Danny and yelled, "Stay on the train, young lad."

CHAPTER 19
OFFICER CERBER HAS DOG BREATH

DANNY WALKED out of the gym with his head held high. Nothing felt better than the hot shower he just had and beating Kevin.

The hallways were crowded with teenagers as everyone headed for the exits. Danny felt a rush of fear when he realized he had no idea what to expect when he walked out of these doors. Ty could be out there waiting for him, and Danny knew he could never kill another man.

I have to talk to Mr. Silen.

Danny pushed through the crowd and headed for Mr. Silen's room. He knew the hippie teacher could guide him in the right direction. He only hoped Mr. Silen would still talk to him after what happened earlier.

Danny froze when he saw Mr. Silen walk out of his room with a large cardboard box. He knew the box was filled with papers and personal items. He remembered what that snake Ms. Echid said:

I should have fired that drunkard years ago.

"Mr. Silen," Danny shouted, waving his arms. "I need to talk to you!"

The teacher turned and opened his mouth, but someone shoved him forward. That's when Danny realized the school security guard Officer Cerber was shoving the teacher toward the exit.

Officer Cerber was six feet tall and looked like someone had smashed his face in with a 2 X 4. His breath always smelled like dead fish. His skin looked like it was bleached and had red pockmarks all over it. He was so ugly and smelled so bad that no one could be around him for more than two seconds without puking.

Officer Cerber glanced back at Danny then seemed to move faster. That's when Danny knew the security guard was a monster. For a moment he had the heads of three dogs and the tail of a snake. He barked at kids and shoved them out of the way, while pushing Mr. Silen forward like an empty shopping cart.

"Wait," Danny shouted.

"You can yell all you want, but you can't make the lines move any faster," William said from behind him. "That's like asking the stars to shine brighter."

Danny knew William would know what kind of creature the officer was. "What has three heads that look like dogs?"

"Please tell me you're kidding."

Danny faced William. "I need to know right now. How dangerous is he?"

William took a deep breath. "That would be Cerberus. He's a hellhound. He guards the entrance and exit of the underworld. His three heads allow him to see the past, present, and future." He looked at the security guard and cleared his throat. "And he only eats live meat."

Danny sighed. Why couldn't any of them be vegetarians? He tried to push through the crowd but it was like a brick wall. He looked back at William. "I'm going to call him Dog Breath."

It seemed like eternity before they reached the exit. The sun and warm air beat down on their faces. Danny didn't see Mr. Silen or the security guard anywhere. "I've got to talk to Mr. Silen. Where is he?"

William pointed ahead to the left.

Danny saw Mr. Silen ten feet away and heading for the parking lot. He took two steps forward and stopped. A huge shadow loomed over him.

"You're not going anywhere," Dog Breath barked with his middle head. He stood in front of them and put his paws out to block Danny in. His fingernails were like razors.

Danny cupped an arm over his nose. The smell was putrid. He stood back and coughed. "You should see someone about that."

Dog Breath barked at him with all three heads.

"What'd he say?" William asked.

Danny remembered that no one else could see or hear what he could. All William saw was the albino with halitosis standing there like a buffoon. "He's not going to let me leave."

"Everything okay?" a female asked as she passed by. Danny forced a fake smile when he realized it was Becky. Marc was by her side and pulled his shirt over his nose.

"Yeah, it's cool," Danny lied. "Just having a conversation with Dog...Officer Cerber."

Becky narrowed her eyes like she didn't believe him at all. "We're still on for tonight, right?"

Danny nodded. "Yeah. Can't wait."

She chuckled in a way Danny had never heard before. It was a genuine laugh, but for a moment he thought it might be flirtatious. She tapped Marc's shoulder and headed out the door.

Marc lowered his shirt and stared up at Dog Breath. "You should be ashamed of yourself! It only costs a dollar or two for floss!" He marched out behind Becky, shaking his head and mumbling.

William slipped out on Marc's far side. He looked back at Danny and mouthed, "I'll stop Mr. Silen."

Danny looked back up at Dog Breath. Something William had said earlier occurred to him. *His three heads allow him to see the past, present, and future.*

"What's going to happen to me when I walk out of this building?" Danny asked.

The hellhound's third head spoke, "Typhon will destroy you."

Danny knew that was a lie. Mr. Silen said the monsters couldn't hurt him. And so far they hadn't.

There was one question he still needed an answer to. "What am I?"

The hellhound's first head spoke, "You're an abomination."

Danny watched as Dog Breath morphed back into the pock marked albino. Danny dodged beneath the guard's lanky arms and headed for the parking lot.

He looked back to make sure Dog Breath wasn't chasing him. The guard stood there with slumped shoulders. Danny remembered that the guard's only purpose was to guard the entrance and exit of the underworld. Did he ever leave?

"I guess it really is hell," Danny said. He turned and raced for the parking lot

Danny spotted William standing by Mr. Silen's sports car and waving him over. Mr. Silen was bent over in the grass, dry heaving.

Danny rushed up to him. "I'm sorry about earlier. I need your help."

"No problem, man," Mr. Silen said. He wiped his lips. "It's been a long, strange trip."

Danny nodded. He looked at William for confirmation. "He said he was a teacher and companion to the gods."

William tapped his fingers on his chin then his eyes brightened. "Silenus…of course! He predated the satyrs and was a tutor to the wine god Dionysus." He stared at Mr. Silen. "You can only teach when you're drunk."

"That's such a dirty word, man. I prefer 'intoxicated.'" He chuckled and shivered. "Which unfortunately I am not right now."

They all turned when someone honked their horn from across the street. Danny felt paralyzed when he recognized the dirty white SUV. The driver's door opened and a familiar face stepped out.

Suit Man.

Danny jumped when Mr. Silen put a hand on his shoulder.

"There is one piece of advice I can give you," Mr. Silen said. "Stay away from him, man."

William stepped forward and squinted. "Who is that?"

Mr. Silen took a deep breath. "That's Jonathan." He leaned in close to Danny and whispered, "Is he okay, man?" He nodded at William.

Danny nodded. "He's helped me figure a lot of things out today. He's okay."

Mr. Silen stepped back. "He's your advisor. Awesome."

Danny motioned toward Suit Man. The guy was leaning against the SUV with his arms crossed. He stuck one arm out and tapped on his watch. Danny didn't need to be reminded that time was running out. "Tell me about Jonathan."

Mr. Silen rubbed his chin. "He's a ufologist and belongs to a society that tracks cosmic masters. He's been studying the stars for years, searching for someone like yourself."

Danny knew Mr. Silen was telling the truth but there had to be more. "He knows about Ty."

Mr. Silen shook his head and sighed. "Jonathan was your age when the monsters attacked us sixteen years ago. His parents were killed during the onslaught."

"They were demigods?" Danny asked.

"His mother was," Mr. Silen said. "You should know that Jonathan has sworn to kill every god and monster."

"Something doesn't add up," William said. "Humans can't see monsters."

Mr. Silen chuckled. "Your advisor is wise, Danny." He reached down and grabbed the box of papers, then grunted and said, "I'm not as young as I used to be."

William snickered. "Exactly how old are you?"

"I stopped counting centuries ago, man." He turned like he was ready to jump in his car and race off.

Danny knew Mr. Silen had stalled for some reason. "How did Jonathan's parents die?"

Mr. Silen froze and stared across the street at Jonathan. "They died trying to save yours."

Danny tried to process what the teacher had said. If Jonathan's parents had tried to save his parents, then why was Jonathan putting pressure on him. Then Danny realized the answer. "He doesn't know who I am."

"It probably doesn't matter anymore. He knows you have the power of the gods. When you used your energy yesterday, he felt it as much as we all did."

Danny froze when he saw the American History teacher Mr. Joyner walk up to Jonathan's van and jump into the back. Jonathan winked at Danny then hopped into the front passenger's seat and waved as they drove away.

Danny put his hands on his head. "What am I supposed to do? Jonathan wants me to kill Ty. He'll kill my parents if I don't. And Ty wants to kill me."

Mr. Silen smiled at Danny. "Be calm, my friend. Go home. I have sent someone ahead of you to help with Ty." He threw the box into his car and slid into the driver's seat.

"Wait," Danny shouted. "What about Jonathan?"

"The gods favor you, Danny," Mr. Silen said. He motioned to William. "Listen to your advisor. Follow your training. No one can hurt you if you believe in yourself."

"My training? What training?"

Mr. Silen closed his car door and rolled the window down. "How are you at sports, man?"

Danny smiled when he remembered the dodge ball battle with Kevin. "I'd say I'm pretty good."

Danny collapsed when something crashed into the side of his head. The world spun as he looked for the culprit. A football lay by his side.

Mr. Silen took off his hippie glasses and put on a pair of shades. He cranked up his car and started to pull away. He stuck his head out the widow and said, "I'd say you might want to work on that."

CHAPTER 20
TRAINING ON THE FOOTBALL FIELD (WITHOUT A FOOTBALL)

DANNY STEPPED into the high school football stadium and stared at the woman on the fifty-yard line, who'd thrown the football at his head. He had never seen her before. She was college age and well tanned. She wore jean shorts and a tank top. If Danny had to rate her on a scale of one-ten, she was a twelve. She was definitely not a monster.

"Today we're going to focus on physical and mental training," she said with an accent he couldn't place.

Danny nodded. "Who exactly are you?"

"My name is Arete. It is my job to help you reach your full potential." She snatched the football from him. "You won't be needing this." She picked a sports bag up from the ground and opened it. She turned the bag over and emptied its contents on the field. Empty soda cans scattered around her.

"Hey, what are you doing?" Danny asked.

Arete arranged the ten cans across the fifty-yard line. "You're going to stand on the thirty-yard line and hit these cans."

Danny laughed. "I didn't bring my BB gun."

Arete marched up to him, grabbed his arm, and dragged him to the thirty-yard line. She turned him to face the cans. "You have to focus on your target. Use your head first." She knocked on his head. "Then use your hands."

Danny shook his head. "I've already tried. This doesn't work. The cans aren't trying to kill me."

She gripped his wrists and held his palms up. "You cannot live by fear or anger. You'll only mess things up. You must use strength, bravery, and knowledge." She shoved his arms down. "Now hit the cans."

Danny watched her take two steps back. Maybe she was right. He widened his stance and threw his arms out.

"No," Arete said. "You're not trying to hit a house. Put your left hand behind your back."

Danny laughed but followed her orders.

"Point your right hand at one of the cans and shoot. Just like a BB gun."

Danny took a deep breath and decided to give it a try. He pointed his palm at a root beer can. He tried to force a ball of energy from his hand but nothing happened.

"I can't do this," Danny said. "No one can. Those aren't real targets."

Arete joined him by his right side. "No one, huh?" She threw out her hands, and small balls of energy volleyed from them at each can on the line. The cans shot up into the air one by one.

Danny closed his mouth, realizing it was wide open. "You're like me?"

She shook her head and said, "I'm whatever I need to be to help you." She looked into his eyes. "What are you fighting for? Focus on that. If you don't have anything to fight for, then you have no reason to fight." She stepped behind him. "Try it again."

Danny thought about his parents. The sun would sink below the tree lines soon, and time was running out to save them. He couldn't let them die, and he had to protect himself. He couldn't be responsible for the destruction of the world.

Danny looked at the scattered cans and slowly put his right hand out. He thought of his mom and dad and how much he loved them. How much they loved him.

The first can flew across the field. The second one fell over when the ground exploded next to it. Danny laughed and put his left hand out. The cans scattered one by one, some when he hit them, others when debris slammed into them.

Danny looked back at Arete and rolled his shoulders back. "Pretty good, right?"

"If you were in class, you'd get an F."

Danny's shoulders dropped. He faced the cans again and prepared to hit them. He stopped when he felt a sting in his left shoulder. He turned and faced Arete. "What the—"

She had a stick in her hand.

"You just hit me with that."

She swung the stick at his other shoulder.

"Ouch! That hurts!"

She threw the stick at him, and he caught it. Arete reached down and picked up another stick.

An odd thought occurred to Danny. "Where are you getting sticks from? We're in the middle of a football field."

She swung her stick at Danny. He blocked it. She swung it harder and faster. "Are you going to fight back or stand there like a little girl?"

"Careful. I don't want to hurt you."

"I can take care of myself. Try to hit me or I'm going to smash your head in."

"What?"

She clobbered the side of his head with her stick.

"All right," Danny said. He swung at her arms the same way she swung at him. She blocked every blow and hit him on the head again. After thirty seconds of this, he realized his couldn't hit her. She was too fast and too strong.

"Widen your stance and control your breathing."

He swung harder.

"Go for the jugular."

"What?"

Arete twirled and pushed Danny down. She stood over him and said, "You won't always have your powers. You must learn to fight like a man. Get up and try again."

Danny stood, centered his balance, and controlled his swing again. The stick seemed to move faster and faster by itself until Arete could no longer block him. Her stick flew out of her hands and across the field.

"Good! Now stop." She put a hand on Danny's shoulder. "When you fight, remember what you're fighting for, Alexandros." She kissed his cheek and smiled. Before she walked away, she said, "When the time is right, use my fire."

CHAPTER 21
MUD IN THE CORNFIELD

DANNY SEARCHED through the crowded festival for Becky that night. He had called her from home, but she didn't answer. After telling his parents most of what happened today, minus the monsters, they let him come as long as he was surrounded by people. Becky said she would meet him here, but he couldn't find her anywhere. Half of the school had come for the Fall Festival. There were games and rides all around. Danny brought his backpack with him for prizes and candy. Most of the kids were in costumes. Danny petted a goat walking through the crowd. It reminded him of Mr. Silen.

"Not cheating on your girlfriend, are you?" Danny looked up at Marc smiling at him. He was slurping down a milkshake.

"Hey, Marc. Sorry about earlier."

"I'm just playing with you. Loosen up, Lover Boy." Marc took the lid off his milkshake and poured some of it into his palm. He put his palm in front of the goat and let it lick his hand.

"Have you seen Becky?" Danny had tried to text her, but the secluded farm was a dead zone for cell service.

Marc giggled and said, "That tickles, you naughty, naughty goat." He wiped his hand on his pants when he saw Danny staring at him. "She was looking for you. She and six of her lady friends went into the corn maze."

"Thanks." Danny headed for the field on the other side of the farm.

"If you hurt her I'll have to kill you," Marc shouted after Danny.

Danny had no doubt Marc was telling the truth. He had always seemed overprotective of Becky. Danny used to think it was annoying, but now he was glad Becky had someone like Marc in her life.

"Wait up," someone said behind Danny. William raced to his side.

"What are you doing here?" Danny asked. He didn't figure William for a guy who liked this kind of fun. He could picture William at a planetarium or museum.

"Are you serious? They hand out candy like it grows on trees." His pockets bulged with candy. "This, of course, is impossible. Candy can't grow on trees. But for one wild night, I'm willing to suspend all belief in reality." He popped a caramel into his mouth.

Danny shook his head and laughed. Maybe William was human after all.

"Where are you going?"

"Corn maze."

Danny stopped when they got to the maze and stared at the posted sign in front of it.

ENTER AT OWN RISK

"I'VE BEEN waiting for you, Alexandros Helen."

Danny looked at the exchange student Aria from Crete. She had a golden complexion and a soothing voice. Most of the guys at school had asked her out, but she said she had a boyfriend back home. She wasn't a monster.

"Rebecca and her friends are in danger."

Danny felt the energy course through his body. He couldn't let anything happen to Becky. He marched toward the corn maze.

"Wait," Aria said. "You will need help." She handed him what looked like the base of a sword.

"What am I supposed to do with this?"

"It is a gift from Hephaestus. Trust your instincts."

William snatched the base from Danny and held it up. His eyes were wide and his mouth agape. "Holy crap." He gave it back to Danny. "Do you know what this is?"

Danny shook his head.

"Okay. Listen." He rubbed his hands together and paced between Danny and Aria. He stopped and pointed at the exchange student. "This is Ariadne, and that," he said, pointing at the corn maze, "is the Labyrinth."

Danny shrugged. "Talk fast."

"Seven went in," Aria said.

"I should have seen this," William said. "The Mino farm. The Minotaur." He popped another piece of candy into his mouth. "Part bull and part man. Trapped inside the Labyrinth. Seven people are sent in each year as a sacrifice." He put his hands on Danny's shoulders. "He eats them."

"How do I stop him?" Danny asked.

"You must cut off his head," Aria said.

"No. There's got to be another way."

William shook his head and looked into Danny's eyes. "I didn't believe it at first. But now I see it. You are a demigod. You have to save them."

Aria stepped up to Danny and kissed his cheek. "Each one of us must slay our own monsters. If we don't, then we can't help the people we love."

Danny turned and raced into the maze. He had to save Becky and her friends. He had to find them in time. "Why do the monsters have to keep eating people?"

"Remember your training," Aria shouted after him. "Use the sword, Alexandros!"

THE GROUND was muddy from last night's rain. The mud splattered on Danny's pants with each step he took. The trail was eight feet wide with corn stalks barricading both sides. This was Danny's first time in a corn maze.

He was twenty feet into the maze when it split off to the right and left. He didn't have time to reach dead ends and make detours. The sign in front of him read:

You could go right
You could go left
You could go blind

You could go deaf

Don't get lost
Don't lose your way
For the cost
Is much to pay

He closed his eyes and raised his arms up by his sides.
"Trust your instincts," he recalled Aria saying.

Danny inhaled and focused his mind on Becky. The
world silenced around him. A burning sensation seared his
right hand. He opened his eyes and saw the top of the wall
of corn stalks on his right was blown back like a strong wind
pressed it down. The power coursed through his body. He
ran like lightning to the next split in the maze. He raised his
arms again and followed his instincts. He was getting closer
to the heart of the maze. Aria said that's where the Minotaur
would be.

He was almost there. He would save them all.

Danny collapsed face first into the mud when someone
or something shoved him from behind. He lifted his face
from the ground and spit out a mouthful of mud. He turned
and looked up to see Kevin's boot aiming for his head.

Danny rolled to his side and swept Kevin's legs.

Kevin plummeted to the mud.

"Kevin, listen to me," Danny pleaded when he jumped
back up.

Kevin rose from the mud and swung at Danny's chin.

Danny stood back, stunned, when Kevin's fist
connected with his jaw. He tasted blood. Danny blocked the
next blow, caught Kevin's arm and flipped him onto his
back. "Don't do this!"

Kevin jumped to his knees. He kicked Danny in the
side.

Danny held his side and fell back. "I don't want to hurt
you! Stop!"

Kevin charged for Danny.

Danny threw out his arms and let a ball of energy shoot at Kevin.

The impact hit Kevin and lifted him a foot off the ground. His body flew backward then hit the mud and slid through it. Kevin didn't move.

Danny stood over Kevin. "This isn't about us. Becky's life is in danger. I need your help."

"Becky?" Kevin turned his head from side to side like he was conflicted and weighing his options. Danny had no idea how Kevin had powers or even why Kevin was after him. Whatever their differences were, it didn't matter right now.

Kevin sat up and put out an arm like he wanted Danny to help him up. Danny didn't trust Kevin, but he did trust that Kevin wanted to protect Becky. He grabbed Kevin's arm and pulled him up.

"For Becky," Kevin said.

CHAPTER 22
THE BEAST AND THE FIRE

DANNY STEPPED into the heart of the corn maze with Kevin by his side. The air was damp and cold. They stared at the mountain of a man with the head of a bull swinging a battle axe over his head. Three of the girls were lined up on one side of the corn stalks. The other four were separated on the opposite side. It would be easy to chop their heads off if they ran for the exits. They all cried and screamed. All of them but Becky.

The beast swung his axe in a wide arc, narrowly missing the girls' necks.

Danny motioned for Kevin to help the girls on the left hand side of the maze. He'd protect the girls on the right. He knew they could get there faster than the beast could swing.

Becky wrapped her arms around Danny when he joined her. "Thank God," she said. "Go get him, Danny."

The beast swung his axe toward Kevin. Kevin leaned back before the blade could decapitate him.

"Hey!" Danny shouted.

The beast turned and raised his arm to swing the axe at Danny.

The power surged through Danny's body. He threw out his arms and fired a ball of energy at the monster.

The beast swung his axe and deflected the energy ball. It shot back toward Danny.

The ball slammed into Danny's gut, and sent him sailing back through the corn stalks. He crashed on his back. Danny stood and brushed himself off. He was unharmed, but it felt like electricity snapped at his body. There had to be another way to stop the monster. He raced back into the opening.

The beast was closer to Becky now. It would be impossible for him to miss. He swung for her head.

"NO!" Danny shouted.

Kevin raced from the opposite side and covered Becky with his body.

Blood flew through the air when the blade slashed through Kevin's back. He collapsed on top of Becky.

Danny couldn't move. He couldn't stop the beast. He couldn't save his friends. The beast had just killed Kevin as he saved Becky's life. All of the girls were screaming.

The beast roared in victory and stood over Kevin with his blade raised above his head. Becky was still beneath Kevin.

Remember your training, Danny heard Aria's voice say in his head.

Danny reached into his backpack and pulled out the sword base Aria had given him. He was supposed to do something with this. It was something Arete had said before she walked away.

When the time is right, use my fire.

Danny felt the power rage through his body and waved a hand over the sword base. A flame shot up from the base to form a complete sword. A fire sword.

Danny raced out of the corn stalks and swung the fire sword at the Minotaur's neck at the same time the Minotaur swung his axe down at Kevin and Becky. The sword sliced the Minotaur's head off with the axe still in the air.

The Minotaur's head plopped off and fell before disappearing with its body. It just evaporated like it never existed.

The six girls ran screaming through the maze.

"Where is he?" Becky said. "Where is Mr. Mino?"

Danny knew exactly where the Minotaur was now. The same place it was before sixteen years ago. "Tartarus."

BECKY CRADLED Kevin in her arms. She held Kevin's head in her lap and cried. Blood trickled from his lips.

"I'm sorry," Kevin whispered. He looked up at Danny. "This is all my fault." His voice was broken.

"Don't talk," Becky said. "Everything's going to be okay. No one can hurt me now. You saved me."

Kevin cried. "I don't wanna die."

Becky held him close and rocked him. "Shhhhh."

Danny felt powerless again. He was supposed to be the protector of the universe, but he couldn't even save his former friend. If it hadn't been for Kevin, Becky would be dead. Danny wasn't sure if Kevin had the ability to heal himself. And who knows? All seven of the girls could have been dead. And what had he become? He had just killed a man. It wasn't right. Things couldn't be any worse right now.

"We meet again, Alexandros Helen." Danny watched as a familiar body stepped out of the cornstalks. The tallest man he had ever seen.

Ty pushed Becky away and clutched Kevin's shoulders. "You failed me," he said to Kevin. "You won't need this anymore." His head shot back like he had been shocked and was absorbing Kevin's power.

"That's the stuff," Ty said with a new surge of energy. He stood and cracked his neck from side to side.

Danny shot his arms out and prepared to attack Ty again. He knew how to use his powers now. Ty would not get up this time.

Ty grabbed Becky and held her in front of him with an arm around her neck. "I wouldn't do that."

"Get him, Danny," Becky said, choking.

By the darkness in Ty's eyes, he wouldn't hesitate to snap Becky's neck. Danny took a deep breath and lowered his arms. "Don't hurt her. I'm right here. Do whatever you want to me."

"That's sweet," Ty said. "Pathetic, but sweet. The boy wants to be a hero." He laughed and backed toward the cornstalks. "But not here. Meet us at the big red barn Alexandros. We'll find out what you're made of."

Ty turned and pushed Becky through the wall of corn stalks with him. Danny raced after them and jumped toward the wall.

The wall turned blue and Danny crashed into it like it was a brick wall. His body slammed into the mud. "What in the world?" He stood and touched the wall. His hand shot away from it like it was an electrical fence.

"Get her back," Kevin said. "You've got to get her back."

Danny looked down at Kevin. He was lying in a pool of blood and barely breathing.

"I can't do this alone," Danny said. His old friend was about to die. The love of his life was in the hands of an evil monster. He couldn't protect his parents. He looked up into the sky and focused on the hidden stars by Polaris. He remembered his birth parents were watching over him.

"Help me!" Danny shouted at the stars.

CHAPTER 23
PARENTAL ADVICE

THE SKY lit up like a flash of sheet lighting, and the two undiscovered stars reappeared. Energy shot out from the stars at the speed of light toward Danny.

Two bodies appeared in front of Danny—one male and one female. They weren't much older than him.

"Look at him," the female said. "He's amazing." She smiled and giggled like Danny was the most incredible thing she had ever seen.

"Hello, son," the man said. His voice was powerful.

Danny felt weak and powerless, like a child. He knew these were his birth parents, and he wanted to ask them a million questions. But he knew time was limited.

"My friend is dying," Danny said, pointing at Kevin. "You have to save him."

His birth mother put a hand on his birth father's shoulder. "He's selfless. Just like his father."

His birth father nodded. "Demigods heal faster than humans, son."

Danny motioned toward Kevin. "He's human."

His birth father stepped up to him. "And you're a demigod." His voice was overpowering. "You can heal him."

"But how?"

His birth father stepped back. "You've done this before." His body began to fade.

"We're proud of you," his birth mother said. Her body began to fade, too.

"Wait! I don't understand!"

"Hold your friends close," she said.

Danny couldn't make sense out of what they told him. And now they were leaving. He wanted to spend more time with them. He didn't have any answers.

"Please don't leave," Danny said.

"We love you, son," his birth mother said.

"Trust Mr. Silen," his birth father said. "Let him be your guide."

The sky flashed again, and they were gone.

DANNY STOOD over Kevin's nearly lifeless body. If Kevin's chest didn't move up and down then anyone would think he was dead. Danny knew how to save him now because of what his birth mother said.

Hold your friends close.

Danny sat in the mud behind Kevin and pulled Kevin's head into his lap. He remembered the cafeteria and what he had done with Bianca. Whatever happened to Bianca? Danny wrapped his hands around Kevin's cold arms and held him close like he was warming his body. The energy built up in his body. He focused his energy on Kevin.

After a few minutes, Kevin jumped out of Danny's lap. "What are you doing?"

Danny laughed. It worked!

Kevin spun around and searched the corn maze walls. "Where's Becky?"

Danny stood and shook his head.

"Typhon has her, man," a familiar voice said, walking into the maze behind Kevin. It was Mr. Silen with Mr. Griffin by his side. "We don't have much time."

Danny nodded at Mr. Silen. "My birth father trusted you, so I trust you."

Mr. Silen nodded back. "I have a couple of things in mind." He took his teashade glasses off and looked at Danny with his bright green eyes. "Gods can do pretty much anything. They're awesome like that." He looked at Kevin. "Even give power back to those who have lost it."

"I'm not a god," Danny said. "I can't do all the things gods can."

Mr. Griffin whistled. "Who you are today is exactly who you believe you are, young lad. Who you are tomorrow is who you believe you'll become."

"I'll do whatever it takes." Danny would give up his life to save Becky. No matter the cost, he would save her.

Kevin stood next to Danny. "Me too."

"It's time to get off the train, young lad," Mr. Griffin said. "You've reached your destination."

CHAPTER 24
SHOWDOWN AT THE BIG RED BARN

DANNY STARED at the big red barn. "You don't have to do this," he said to Kevin.

Kevin stood by his side and stared with him. "Yes I do." He put a hand on Danny's shoulder. "Are you sure this is gonna work?"

Danny nodded. "It has to." He stepped forward and headed for the barn entrance. The plan wasn't perfect but he would do whatever he had to do to save Becky. Mr. Silen had advised him to use his power to give Kevin his power back. So he did. Kevin had sworn to use it only to help save Becky.

Danny froze when they entered the barn and held Kevin back. Kevin's body tensed as they looked upon Becky's body strung up with chains hanging from the barn ceiling. She was ten feet off the ground.

"Let's have a chat, Alexandros," Ty said, standing beside Becky now. On the other side of Becky were Frog Lady, Snake Lady, and the Sphinx.

"I thought she was dead," Kevin said to Danny, pointing to the Sphinx.

The Sphinx laughed. "Human weapons cannot hurt gods or monsters. I have a riddle for you, Kevin Skinner."

"No thanks."

"What's black and blue and bloody all over? I'll give you a hint: it's you after I tear you apart."

Ty held out a hand for the Sphinx to be silent. "I'm going to make this easy for you, Alexandros." He looked up at Becky. "Her life or your life."

Danny knew he wouldn't hesitate to give up his life for Becky's. But it wouldn't do any good. If Ty killed him then Ty would get all of his powers back and wipe out the world.

"Let go of me," Kevin said. "We can take them."

Snake Lady hissed and laughed. "You can't beat us. There's only one god in this room." She nodded at her husband Ty. "Besides, there are four of us and only two of you."

"Make that three," a female's voice said from behind Danny.

"No," Frog Lady screamed. "You'll be meatloaf next week."

A teenage female with a bouncy ponytail stepped next to Danny's side and crossed her arms. Mr. Silen had brought her here. It was the school's reporter Bianca.

Danny shot a ball of energy at Ty. "Keep them away from Becky," he shouted at Kevin and Bianca. They raced toward the monsters.

Danny's feet lifted off the ground. Ty held a hand out toward his body and balled his hand into a fist. Danny felt like his body was being crushed.

From here he could see Becky. She was still safe. Kevin and Bianca must have contained the monsters.

"Get him, Danny," he could see Becky mouth to him.

Energy was building inside him again. He yelled and threw his arms out. He broke free of the invisible hold Ty had on him. He shot out his arms and fired ball after ball at Ty.

Ty waved his hands from side to side and deflected the energy balls. The energy fired like cannon balls in every direction, busting holes into the barn walls and knocking over farming tools.

Danny ran toward him with balls still shooting out.

Ty deflected them at record speed.

Danny stopped in front of Ty, and the energy built in him stronger than it had before. A ball of energy the size of his body formed in front of him. He pushed it forward to take Ty out once and for all.

Ty held out his hands and pushed the ball back. It was suspended between them now, both of them pushing with all of their might, knowing that whoever lost would be sent to Tartarus.

"Danny!" Becky shouted.

Danny turned and saw the Sphinx jab a pitchfork into Becky's side. The huge ball of energy hit Danny and sent him flying back through the barn walls.

Danny couldn't move. His body felt numb, paralyzed. He was too late. Becky would be dead.

"Gods and monsters can't die by human weapons," Ty said, standing over him. "But humans can. What a shame."

Ty reached down and pulled something out of Danny's backpack. He studied it and smiled. It was the fire sword base. "The gods favor you, but they can't help you now."

Danny laughed. "I'm going to cut your head off."

The barn roof crashed in like a meteor hit it. Wood splintered over the entire barn. The massive Griffin swooped in and snatched Becky's body. He roared and flew off.

"No!" Ty shouted. "It's not possible!"

Danny smiled as the Griffin flew off into the night. Mr. Silen had convinced Danny that he could give power back to those who lost it. He had laid his hands on Mr. Griffin and focused on the man's internal strength. It took complete concentration, but the result was amazing. Mr. Griffin was now the Griffin again, in all his greatness.

"Anything's possible," Danny said. He was standing behind Ty now. He snatched the sword base from Ty and waved his hand over it. The flame shot out. Danny smirked at Ty's blank expression and sliced his head off.

THE GRIFFIN flew back into the barn and lay Becky's body down. He hovered over her to keep her body warm. She was nearly motionless, but her chest seemed to move up and down every few seconds. Blood gushed from her side where the Sphinx had stabbed her.

Danny raced to Becky's side. Kevin and Bianca stood back weeping.

"No," Danny said. "Not like this." He sat behind her with tears in his eyes and held her the same way he had held Kevin and Bianca. All of his power went into her.

Her body was as cold as Bianca's was in the freezer. Her chest wasn't moving anymore. Danny held her tighter.

"Please work!"

Danny felt Kevin put a hand on his shoulder. "It's too late," Kevin said. "You did everything you could."

Danny stood and shoved Kevin down. "Don't tell me it's too late! You don't know anything!"

"Danny," Bianca said. "Do something."

"This can't be it," Danny cried. He stared down at Becky's lifeless form. "I don't know what else to do."

Gods can do pretty much anything, Mr. Silen's voice echoed in Danny's head. *They're awesome like that.*

Danny huffed. "I'm not a god."

Who you are today is exactly who you believe you are, Mr. Griffin's voice echoed. Danny looked up at the mighty creature hovering over Becky. The Griffin nodded its head and cawed.

Danny knelt by Becky's side and squeezed his eyes shut. He inhaled and felt the power build inside him like a volcano. His body quaked as he raised his palms by his sides.

We're always there for each other, Becky's voice echoed.

The energy exploded from Danny's hands and appeared as fire shooting out from his palms.

The Griffin roared.

Danny opened his eyes and looked back and forth at his hands. He flipped his hands over, with the fire shooting toward Becky's body.

He put his hands on Becky's wounds and let the fire shoot inside of her until he was too weak to sustain it.

The wounds were gone but Becky didn't move. Danny looked up at Kevin and Bianca. "It didn't work. I failed."

Bianca had a hand over her mouth.

Kevin's eyes were wide.

Danny looked back down at Becky. Her eyes fluttered and opened. "You're the best thing that's ever happened to me, Danny Neumann."

CHAPTER 25
FRIENDS FOREVER

DANNY SAT at the school lunchroom table with his friends the next day. Not the phonies who partied with him on the beach. These were his real friends. Becky, Kevin, William, and Bianca.

They had all stood with him last night when he faced Jonathan after killing Ty. Jonathan believed him when he surveyed the damage in the barn. They told him that Snake Lady, Frog Lady, and the Sphinx were still out there. He thanked them and said he'd take care of it.

"What about my parents?" Danny had asked.

"Don't worry, Danny boy," Jonathan said. "Your parents are safe. No one's going to hurt them."

Danny took a deep breath and focused on his friends. "We make a great team."

Bianca wiped a crumb off William's lips. "Yes we do." She untied her ponytail and let her hair drape over her shoulders.

William stared at her like she was the Nobel Prize. "Unequivocally."

Danny laughed and shook his head. He had a feeling about these two. "Get a room."

Mr. Griffin walked by with a broom. "I hope you enjoyed the train ride, young lad. There's always some place new to go." He winked.

Danny nodded when Mr. Griffin tipped his hat. The janitor was the only being now who could choose to be a man or a creature. He was the most powerful creature Danny had ever seen. If only Danny had listened to Mr. Silen sooner then maybe half of what happened yesterday wouldn't have happened. He wouldn't make that mistake again.

"What do we do now?" Kevin asked.

Danny wasn't sure. Snake Lady, Frog Lady, and the Sphinx were still out there. They dispersed when Ty was sent back to Tartarus. None of them came back to school today. Even Dog Breath wasn't polluting the hallways. Danny suspected he would never see them again. They didn't have a leader, and they knew he was more powerful than them.

"They're still out there," Danny said. He stood and looked around at his friends. "We train our bodies, our powers, and our hearts. The day will come again when the fate of the world is in our hands. We are protectors of the universe."

William raised his hand. "The universe? That could take a while. There are four thousand—"

"Shut-up," Bianca said, shaking her head. "I'm going to get a really good story out of this."

Danny sat back down and sighed.

Becky leaned over and nudged her shoulder against his. "You're amazing, Danny Neumann."

Danny smiled. That was what his birth mother had said. "You're pretty amazing yourself."

"Hey," someone said from behind Danny. "Did you guys form a new club and leave me out of it?" The high pitched voice was unmistakable. It was Marc.

Marc snatched an empty chair from the next table over and shoved it between Danny and Becky. "Move over, Lover Boy. You're not leaving me out of this."

Danny looked around Marc at Becky. She giggled and nodded at him. Danny knew Marc would do anything to protect Becky. Maybe it wasn't a bad idea.

Danny looked at his friends. They all nodded. "Marc, if you want—"

Marc held up a hand. "Oh, I want. Now make it happen."

They all laughed and talked amongst themselves. Bianca had a great idea for a story. William tried to convince her to write about something with science. Kevin kept apologizing to Becky. It was clear that the two of them were done, but would work on being friends. Becky winked at Danny. He wondered where their relationship would go from here.

Sure, they were all dysfunctional, but he couldn't ask for better friends.

CHAPTER 26
THE NAME ON THE MAILBOX

ECHIDNA STOOD on the sidewalk in front of a cozy three-bedroom brick house. She watched through the front window as a middle aged man and woman sat down for a hot lunch. It looked like they were about to eat baked chicken leg quarters and mashed potatoes.

"It's time," she said to the Sphinx, Lamia, and Cerberus.

She walked toward the front door, knowing they were close behind. She didn't grieve her husband's death. He had escaped from Tartarus once. He could do it again.

Echidna looked at the gas cans in her daughter's hands. The matches were in her pockets. It was time to play with fire. Echidna rang the doorbell then turned and looked at the mailbox. "It's a shame," she said to Lamia. "I'm sure they're nice people."

Echidna smiled when the door opened and took one last look at the name on the mailbox.

NEUMANN

THE END...for now.

ABOUT THE AUTHOR

I don't believe in monsters, but I sleep with the sheets over my head. I hate getting wet, but I stay in the shower until the hot water runs out. I never drive over the speed limit, but I like to race cars. I'm a good listener, but I talk a lot in my sleep. I'm not a bad person, but I write to free my demons.

Timothy D. McLendon lives in Orlando, Florida with his beautiful wife Regina and his fiery son Zander Blaze.

www.tdmclendon.com

Made in the USA
Lexington, KY
25 March 2016